The Bastardo

A literary tale of the Sicilian Mafia, the beginning.

By Steve Kravetz

ISBN: 978-0-9996355-5-1 [SC]

ISBN: 978-0-9996355-6-8 [E]

Published by Steve Kravetz

Cover design: Steve Kravetz// Art work by:

jbinspiration@fiverr

Preface

In the 1850's a perfect storm came to Sicily. The Royalty had been over thrown. The old ways of governing where absentee land owners depended on middle men to oversee rent collection and to handle day to day issues were coming to an end.

With no one to protect these large rural estates from theft, kidnappings and extortion, the owners were forced to hire private armies to protect their assets and lease holders.

Add the fact that every navy and sailing ship that floated had a need for lemons and the number one place they grew this yellow, golden fruit was Sicily. Large profits were to be had by those who controlled this much needed commodity. Sicily's fertile grounds produced lots of cash and lots of opportunities for those who were strong enough to control a part of that market.

The Bastardo

"I will always remember this day forever. It was when my past crashed into the future, to create the purpose for my present." Tomaso, "Masso", De la- Rosa, 1855.

A baby boy was found in the early morning hours of August 18, 1843, at the front gates of the Villa De la Rose in the *Enna* province of *Sicily*. His dark green eyes looking out inquisitively from the interior of the picker's basket. The child, a month or so old, was bare to the world except for a small metal of Saint Tomas of Arimathea, around his thin neck. The boy's carpet of dark red hairs was just starting to cover his large head. The mysterious baby was immediately adopted by the estate and given the name Tomaso for his Saint. Though, he was forever to be known as, Masso.

Early morning hours in the stables of the La Barbra's estate before Masso finds his destiny.

"Masso, where have you been? The Don is leaving and requested to see you before he goes and you have already kept him waiting too long. Hurry up now," said Father Stefano stressfully.

"What does the Patron want with me, Father?" The boy asked eagerly.

"You ask me like I know what Don Leonardo thinks, just get moving and don't ask questions that will be answered soon enough," replied the village's old priest , Father Stephano.

The fact was, until four years earlier the Don had spoken fewer than twelve words total to the boy, but then so much had happened in these last forty- eight months.

The change came by accident, during one of Masso's explorations in the gardens. He found the hidden door in the wall, behind an old cypress tree. There, Masso found an iron decorative piece in front of the old wood panel. Only upon closer inspection would anyone ever notice the wood pieces were, in fact, a door. Hidden to the side, Masso found a simple wood peg lever which when pulled opened. It freed the weathered wood door on its old iron hinges, squeaking as they cracked, opening inward. What he found was an unknown passage way between the walls that surrounded the house. Dank and musty odor filled Masso's nose. Curiosity the boys felt, was a bigger motivator to his burning urges than fear of an unknown. As he walked into the empty space Masso noticed the way was lit by sunlight streaming though gaps in the rock walls. It was as if the mortar had been deliberately missed in certain areas, to allow for this illumination. Masso followed the passage which led back to the villa and to a small set of step, to another large wood panel with a similar wood lever as the hidden gate door.

When Masso pulled the handle down that day he had no idea where it would lead or how it was going to change his life, forever. The whole panel swung in, and as he stuck his red wooly head into the newly reveled space. What he was looked into was a room full of books. There were shelves and shelves of them along two of the walls floor to ceiling, more books than he had ever though existed in the whole world. An as the young curious boy stepped deeper into the room, what he was able to see there, were maps and paintings covering the other wall spaces. Old iron weapons were lying around in piles here and there and even two strange covering suits of armor were in a corner. One made of iron the other looked to be made of some kind of round wood pieces.

 A heavily ornately carved wooden desk sat in the middle of the large window which looked out on to the gardens. Flowers on the left side, vegetables on the right, and beyond them began the forest of lemon trees, all the way down to the road, like a village of wooden men, with yellow and green hair.

"This must the Don's special place." Masso thought to himself as he walked around the large room, he was trying to take in as much as he could.

From the beginning the Don had appointed Masso's care to Augusto, the estate manager along with his wife Mella, the mid-wife and herbalist for the area.

Masso had never been further inside of the villa than the kitchen. His closest interior views had been while he looked through the windows as he cleaned them from the outside. He made it regularly into the kitchen only because one of his jobs was to supply meat and fowl to the estates kitchen when the Don was in residence.

 Masso had been going into the woods and hills to hunt for roots or flowers with Mella since as far back as he could remember. She would bring him to help dig up plants, giving him her knowledge of their benefits and dangers of each of the plants parts. It was from these early days that Masso learned to observe the wild life that was around them and where his skills with his sling shot were honed. Soon enough anything walking, crawling, or even flying was not safe from his leather and stone. He would bring fresh killed meat or fowl from the previous night's hunt, to the manors back door.

 Don Leonardo had always been a generous Patron. He provided for the entire village a tutor, at least for a few months every year, during the off season. Anyone who wished to learn to read, write, and to gain basic math skills was encouraged to attend.

Masso started attending classes at age four where the tutor opened his mind to the world outside the orchards and area farms. Then Padre Stefano was the teacher of God and his Son's words on Sundays. His teachings also included some Latin.

Masso's first visit to the library was just a short look around, a scouting adventure. The boy's natural curiosity was too great though. So from that day on Masso kept finding himself being drawn back. Inside were books with stories and ideas and knowledge Masso had never dreamed or considered. *The Don must be the smartest and luckiest man to have ever lived,* Masso thought. *The Don has gotten to read all these many books and now has all their knowledge in his head*. So too the young boy began reading. Each new book opened another world and his fertile mind. Masso consumed them as a thirsty man who finds water well in the desert. With his eyes now beginning to open, Masso could he see how many smart men are actually were out in the world and each has a different way of seeing things.

Late one night when the eight year old thought everyone had gone to bed he slipped though the swing door, as he done many times before. This time though Masso found the Don sitting at his desk, busy in thought. Don Leonardo too was quite startled by the boy and by the unexpected intrusion of his space.

Masso quickly turned and tried to leave, but.

"Come back here boy, what are you doing here, how did you find the passage?" His gruff voice did shake the boy's confidence a little.

Though Masso was afraid, the thought he could be prohibited from coming back or worse, sent away, was greater. So Masso slowly turned back to face this looming figure at the desk.

"I found the way from the garden many months ago and I come here to learn. I promise I have taken nothing but words and thoughts Sire. I will leave you to your business as you wish Sir." Masso wanted to run as fast as he could but took a few breaths then began to turn, when he heard the old man's voice. Now with a little softer tone.

"No come in, sit down there Masso," the Don pointed to old leather chair next to his desk. "And what are you reading if I may ask? What catches your interest?" The old man asked sincerely.

"Well sire there is so much to learn at first I would try to read several books at once. Now I try to just read one at a time and concentrate on what its saying. Lately it has been Niccol Machiavelli's book, *The Prince*, do you know it?"

"His ideas are pretty strong, forceful. Do you understand what he is trying to say, Masso?"

"He is just repeating what goes on in the real world, of nature. A rabbit has speed, flexibility and in his brambles he is safe. He has all the food he needs just a jump or two away, but if he comes out, the hawk that has stealth and patients, can produce fatal force. And when he catches his prey in the open the hawk now has the advantage over the rabbit. Might equal's right in the end one is the winner the other the dinner."

"Yes, that is the blood and meat of it," he said chuckling. "And what will you do with all this knowledge Masso?"

"Knowledge, I read somewhere, is power itself something you can never have too much of, something you can't lose and you can take it with you no matter where you go."

"Yes knowledge can bring great power and wealth if used correctly but it also brings great burdens and responsibilities. Choices, hard choices like would you rather be loved or feared?" The old Don was testing him out.

"What's love? I know that if you give to the land your time and energy. That land will give back to you all you need. I do have control of who I am, what I do. I like me and that's enough for now. I never really considered any one fearing me, but I do like the idea; FEAR, the concept certainly has power."

"Yes it does, and you I believe, in time will find how to best use it to your advantage. Don't ever be weak boy and, do it quickly, forcefully, and never regret your decisions. For you will know when it will be right for the time." A moment of silence was shared between them before the Don spoke again. "If you wish I will recommend a few books to expand your course of study. From there we will see."

"Thank you Patron, I value your opinion as well the concerns and interest in this poor son of Del la Rosa."

The next forty eight or so months found the boy busy 18 hours a day. Masso was working his normal duties during the days. Then at night with or without the Don, Masso was studying works of Aristotle, Plato, and Leonardo De Vinci. It was an ancient warrior teacher from the other side of the world which would have the most profound way of viewing life that he found most compelling. The authors name was *Sun Tzu* a Chinese General who wrote the book, *Art of War*, almost 2400 years earlier. Each one of the thirteen chapters was devoted to different aspect of war fare and how it applies to strategy and tactics. Masso saw it as a way to deal with everyday life as well.

 The boy was surprised to learn that his new educational curriculum was not just going to be limited to books. The Don made sure his student had hands on experiences. He learned for one to shoot armaments of all types. Masso also learn the use of steel weaponry from swords, to picks and pikes. One of Masso's most important and fun lessons was his field artillery training. What boy does not get excited by blowing things up? Though the cannon he was using was a small bronze one, off an old ship, previously used for communication. When loaded with shot or rocks would give him the feel of what its big brothers could really do. It was all about getting use to the calculation of angle, plus wind, plus charge equal distance.

 Though it was the use of a simple wood staff that caught the boy's interests the most. With calculated moves, though the quickest and simplest of actions. Masso could be quite deadly. He even began developing his own style in winning the face to face combats.

The Don also made sure the young student read about agriculture especially about crop bearing trees and vine growing fruit. The Don wanted Masso to be able to use every bit of these new proven ways to improve Del La Rosa's Lemmon trees production, and that of the other trees and vineyards.

Don Leonardo would from time to time take Masso on field trips as he would call them. The first was to a friend's estate. Don Delfino's estate was four times the size of La Rosa. Most of the trees were Lemon trees. They were taking over most of the estates grow space, followed by the vineyards and a few olives trees. Masso was hoping he could explore it all first hand, by himself. One thing Masso noticed immediately about Don Tito Delfino's place was how immaculate clean it was. The first view he remembered the most, trees upon trees lined up in rows. Each standing tall, looking like an army of defenders. The trip was meant as a learning experience for Masso .

When they arrived Masso was introduced as the Don's valet, but Masso felt they probably knew the truth. Don Tito had two children as Masso would meet on his arrival.

"Lucia, take Masso down to the stables and get him settled in. Then if you would, show him around. I think he'll be impressed with what we have done. "Don Tito askes his thirteen year old daughter, who in truth was the old man's right hand and pride and joy.

"Si, Poppa. Come this way. What did you say your name is, boy?" Lucia asked? Her tone was openly friendly?

"Masso, "But before he could say more, Enrico her younger brother, came around the corner.

"What you got here Miss Toady. It looks like you got stuck with the Don's bastardo. Imagine that, not one but two losers in one spot," giggling out loud as he ran off.

She said nothing but just seemed to lose herself, just continued to walk toward the stables at the bottom of the hill. She was embarrassed and angry and could not hold back the feeling and tears run down her cheek. Lucia was not a very pretty young woman. Her features were more masculine and she inherited a large dark mole on an ear and a few bumps on her face.

"Here take a drink of water," Masso reached into his pack and handed her his canteen of water. She reached out and opened the top and took a deep swallow choking a little on too much water. Lucia handed the canteen back as he asked.

"Is the bottle half empty, or half full?" Seconds ticked by as she starred at him not sure exactly, what he say, or what he mean? Then like a candle being lite in a dark room it hit her, what it was he asked and even more, why?

Masso saw it, in her dark black eyes too.

"Lucia, we have no control of where we are born, who our parents are. We can't change what color we are, or how we look, but we do have control of, is what we do with ourselves and our lives."

Lucia just stared at him not knowing what to say. Unexpectedly she found Masso a challenge. Though most of their conversation that day was mostly about the trees and the techniques they used to get the results. He wanted to know if they had tried this or that, as he had read about or used on the Don Leonardo's own orchards. *He does not engage in idle chatter but when he did speak his questions were well thought out. When he gives his option his words are worth listening to. His face is of a kid but his poise and intelligence comes forward as quite a force, even at his young age. Who is this boy/man*, she asks herself?

Months would pass before another trip. This one was to the small port town of *Agrigento* on the west coast. They went to meet some of the Don's partners on a shipping firm operating out of this small port. It was the first time Masso had been to a city bigger than *Caltanissetta*. His first taste of urban living, a city with large busy markets, and with more people in one place then he had ever seen before or knew existed. His role was to listen and observe how business was being done and at the end of the day they would discuss what he had seen and get questions answered.

The trip Masso found the most interesting was to meet both of the Don's and Father Stefano's extended families. The port of *Massing* was the closest to Italy's main land, and while *Palermo* was where the business actions were created for buying and selling commodities. *Massing* was where the real actions took place, the shipping of those products. The Don's younger brother Arturo and his sons Alberto and Antonio took care of that end of the family's trading business. Arturo's family was also responsible for all the family's accounting. The last member of the family was Arturo's oldest son Arturo the Third, who was currently serving in the military.

"What's the boy doing here Leo? Have you gotten so feeble you need a nurse mate brother?" The smaller and younger version of the Don asked as he lovingly hugs his big brother.

"This is my body guard if you must know, and he is quite deadly with a sling shot." The old Don joked. "Now Arturo how serious is this crisis Francis and his uncles have gotten us into this time?" The two went in company's offices in the warehouse to finish their discussion, and as he left, the Don nodding for Masso to stay there.

Ever full of curiosity the lad wandered the property watching the crews load skiffs with wooden barrels of spoiled lemon juice and brine, waste from the juice processing. On the other side of the docks were the incoming fresh citrus harvest of oranges, limes and the family's own lemon crop. Late that night as everyone else was asleep Masso was back in the shadows of the wharf watching, and observing and thinking to him-self. *A lot of this fruit is not making on board. It appears* to *be going into the water*. On the other side of the ship were small row boats. Who were busy netting the floating fruit and putting it into their *own boat*. When full it would slowly row away the next one ready to replace it… *'X lira per day times Y number of days equals a lot of money, add how many ships are coming through this just this one port. The loss could be serious money.* Masso's mind begins working on new angles.

The next morning's destination was to the offices of Father Stefano's two siblings. The La Barba's family's bankers, and the priest Stefano's two brothers, Hector and Felix Goldin. Introductions were not made but Masso was allowed to sit in a chair while the family's' financial business was being discussed.

The trip home latter that day found the two in dead silence. The old man was deep in thought. Masso was doing his best, just to hold his tongue. Finally the boy could no longer sit on the question that had been baffling him for quite a while. "Sir, how can you work so hard to get the most out of our trees, and then give away the fruits of our land, for a loss? Why have you not stepped back in sir and…?"

The old man looked at the boy, wondering to himself, *how much to tell*. "There is more here than what appears on the surface Masso. Some debits, old ones, are paid not in cash but other obligations, and they too have to be paid."

Masso with only half the information given, understood. He also knew this was not the time to push or to discuss what else he had observed, *another day another time*, he thought to himself.

The lads' first solo assignment was given to him by the Don himself when he was ten. "Masso, I'm sending you to pay this year's water charges, to Senior Allaya."Don Leonardo explains patiently.

The Allaya family was one of the founding families in this area of the province. Their clan it is said came here in the early 1700's and hand dug the underground source of the water that feed the reservoir. It was shortly after that the family began selling excess water. In an area where rain fall was always never enough and this source of water made the land all around more valuable and useful. The Allaya family provided the water for much of the area's agriculture and live livestock needs. The agreement was that at the end of harvest season the year's water bill was due.

Masso met with the Don early the next morning.

"Put this pouch of silver in your leather pack and deliver it promptly to Don Allaya himself. No one else, then be sure to get a receipt. And don't be side tracked by anything else, do you understand?"

He had been to the area many times with Mella, hunting plants that only grew around water.

"Yes Sire, I know the way, there and back."

"Don Allaya only, and be sure you get a receipt."

He would always remember how very proud of himself he felt, that Don had chosen only him to do this very important task without any help.

The journey was uneventful and he made it to the midpoint, the cross roads known s," four points," where one road left back toward town the other to the lake and Don Allaya's. Two men Masso did not recognize were waiting. One in his early 20's thin, poorly dressed and for some reason he looked mad and worked up. The second man was a little older, heaver and smelled like he had been sleeping with chickens.

"Where do you think you're going, Shepherd boy?" asked the younger man with an attitude.

Without replying, Masso attempted to move around them, but for each move he made the young guy and his buddy countered.

"I am not going to ask you again you little sheep fucker?" The man speaking moved to grab him with his right hand. A large knife now appeared in the left. Masso quickly moved out of this man's grasp and as he looked to his left, the fat friend attempted to come from behind him.

The end of Masso's staff found its mark in the middle of the slow-moving fat man's noise. The sound the fat man made was first the crunching of cartilage, then moaning and gasping for breath. The only other sound that was heard at that moment was the iron wood hawk slicing through the still air until it smacked down on its prey. The left knife bearing arm of the advancing man's elbow, again the sound of bone and cartilage cracking filling the air. The whistling of the wood passing through the air for a second time before it delivered its damaging blow to the advancing man's right knee. The only noise heard now was the voices of two screaming men. The young warrior never turned or looked back. His task was not yet complete.

That day, Masso learned for himself a valuable lesson. Under conflict he would not run and he could and would do whatever it takes to complete his goals.

"Did you have any problems on you delivery Masso?" the Don asked him when he returned with the receipt latter that day.

"No sir, all went as planned."

The months went by like falling hail, faster and faster as it moved downward towards the ground. With each month came challenges, and a few failures but mostly successes. When problems came, Masso always seemed to find a way to deal with them. The soon to be thirteen year old Masso, was a force to be reckoned with.

Destiny -1856

"Good morning Don Leonardo, "Masso greeted his Don, "I am sorry I have kept you waiting, Padre Stefano said you needed to see us?"

Greeting them that morning was a different man. Don Leonardo La Barbra's whole presence seemed to have change over a matter of hours. Like the air of confidence he always had, was gone. Looking back at us was now an older and very tired looking patron.

"Both of you come in and shut the door. I have to go to a meeting later today. I have no idea how it is going to end so now before I leave I want to put in place a contingency plan. You both know I have been working on putting a 'Citrus Union,' together for years. In doing so I did not have time for everything. One of the things I negated was the families business. I gave the day to day running of the La Barba trading company to Francis and my two brother's In-laws. Not totally my choice, but obligations are being met. In ancient times Royal families had close retainers whose own families' lines served for life those Royal families. They would go so far as to sacrifice their own lives to do what was best for their families they served. In certain circumstances, like the head of the house dies or becomes incapacitated, or if the families next in line was too young or not able to do the job. It was then, a retainer who had been appointed by the families to the position as **Abortrador**. The **Abortrado**r has the last word on all family business, from marriage choices, to how the family runs business or investments were and when dispersed. He was to keep all members of family informed, offer advice if requested. Listen to both sides of any disagreement between family members and make a final decision on what's best for the whole family, period. He was the Don, in spirit, until the old Don takes back control, or a new Don is appointed. I believe Masso your only interest is what will be best for the whole La Barba family. Circumstances being what they are I am appointing you the La Barbra's family Arbortrador. I give you, should the family need you, the absolute power in disputes and your decisions are law per the code. I have set up a small independent account at our bank for you and it will sustain your independence. Even though you are young, I have faith in your love for our land and will do whatever that is needed to protect her and our family. Father Stefano and I have had many discussions on the family's future, so feel free to use him for advice if I'm not around. Do you accept this commission?"

"Certainly sir, but is this discussion to lead me to believe you think you may not be coming back sir?"

"Just a precaution Masso, times are a changing and we must be as prepared for it as much as we can. We must keep all options open don't you think? Besides you know one never knows when any of our enemies will appear or set a trap."

A Month Later

 "Wake up Masso, we must talk, hurry wake up," Stefano, yells at Masso as he tries to shake him awake.

 "It is too early this morning father, I've barely been down. Nothing we need to talk about that at least a couple hours delay will not keep. I just got in and need a few, in the morn."

 "No you don't have until the morning and we have much to do over the next few hours. The Don was ambushed after his meeting last month we are just finding out. It is not good he is in a catatonic state, not dead but not functioning. Frances had taken the opportunity to take over control of everything and putting his uncle on notice."

"Where is the Don now? Is he under protection? How could this have happen, why?" The boy with deep concern asked as he hurriedly got dressed.

"He is in *Palermo*, being looked after, and not a real threat to any one now. I guess he was in conflict with another faction over his Union thing. They did not like what he had to offer and saw him as an obstacle to their own plans. Someone tried to garrote him shortly after the meeting. The old man was able to fake death before it really came and survived. Luckily for the Don, the assassin was weak and sloppy. For now, he lives, if you can call it that. The bad news is, I just got. Frances has leased this estate and the new owner wants everyone out. For you, Frances has gone all out. He conscripted you to the Army and they too are due to pick you up shortly."

"Me in the Army, why the army?"

"Money of course, you were lucky the Army paid him more for your body than the sulfur mines were paying for their fresh meat boys. Masso, you could have just as easily become one of those poor souls, having to go down into the bowels of the earth every day. So we need to empty as much of the families stuff as possible before the new owner take over. His library and office are where most of the important stuff is, so in there we shall start. Go to the stables and hook up the large cart to a couple horses and meet me at the garden wall passage"

The next several hours found them loading art, maps, armament including the Japanese wooden war out fit with a fierce face mask and tight woven wood dowel armor and their two swords. As many of the families' books and records. They also found some legal notes obligations that were owed to the Don and were to be paid upon demand. His desk had hidden compartments some they both had seen open but this was a specially made piece of furniture. In side one of the hidden chambers the father found the Don's personal diary. They took as much as the two could load in the short time they had. These items of real value were put and store it in the basement of the church. The space was also the Padres private sleeping quarters. It did bring a bit of improve to his previous barren space.

Masso last night was spent restlessly wondering the estate trying to absorb all that he saw into his memory, and really did not waste time on,' what was to be, he knew it will come.' He would just have to deal with it as it came.

The boy had only a few hours of rest before the four Sardinian Army soldiers came by to pick him up where he joined six others in the back of a wagon going no one knew where.

"Driver we have been on this wooden box you call a wagon 6 hours now, can we get a break to relieve ourselves, maybe walk a few miles to stretch out legs?" Masso asked as his bladder had needed to be emptied two hours ago.

The old man driving the wagon just kept looking forward like he was not there. The Sargent sharing his bench, stood up and said, "you are in the Army now, and the Army will tell you when you will walk, when you will sleep, when and what you eat and when and where to shit. So shut your mouths up and do what your told when your told, do you shit's understand, well do you?"

The group all just nodded saying nothing for the rest of the trip, which ended at the port city of *Trapani* to be loaded on to a sailing ship with his 6 mates and about 50 other men and boys. They found themselves spending the night and most of the day being thrown around like cheap freight; most of the group looked green and spent much of the journey hanging on to a wood bucket or the railings of the ship. The new recruit's destination was to be the west side of the Island of *Sardegna* and the port city of *Alghero*. From there they departed and spent the next day walking to the encampment.

Masso's assigned duties were assist the companies' cook, a job that did not require a uniform, a weapon, or any real skills, *it's a beginning*, he thought so, *and I'm going to be the best cooks' assistant any army has ever had.*

"Recruit Masso reporting for service Sergent."

The sight before Masso was a 5'3' grizzly of a man who's age could be anywhere from 40 to 80. The hairy old cook must have weighted close to 200 pounds. The sergeant had many red broken blood vessels on his face that told a story of an alcoholic. But it was his swollen bulbous nose that told it all. This man had been on the losing side more than one hand- to-hand combat. He glanced as he stood up from his fire. The boy knew he was looking him over as if he was just another hunk of fresh meat he was consider buying. First he grabbed Masso's hands in his, turning them over as to judge the character of the body that stood before him. Next he grabbed the boy's hair pulling his head back then sticking his fingers into the youth's mouth to look at his teeth.

"You'll do boy, put your gear in the tent closest to the wagon over there."

"Sure sergeant, let me put my bag away then I will ready for whatever you need, yes sir." nodded his head as he walked off to store his gear and he was back in just a few moments. "I have two arms ready for work, what do you want me to do cookie?" Masso asked eagerly, as he ran up.

"Slow down kid there is plenty for you to do. See those hills up there?" I turn to see where he is pointing, and just nod. "We need firewood, so go up and bring back as much as you can, understand? I always need firewood. So any time you're free, get firewood. They too, always need cleaning. When you're done with that, come back and see me and I'll find something else for you to do." The old warrior smiled to himself. *We got us another gung-ho recruit, at least for a while.*

The road that led into camp followed around several wooded hill areas. Masso had not been in his first stop but a few moments when a familiar movement caught his eye, by reflex the boy had his sling out winding and hurling at his target, tonight' s dinner for someone. In a few hours' time, the newest cook's assistant had bagged three rabbits and picked and dug enough fresh greens and edible roots to make a feast, plus the collected firewood.

When Masso finally did return, he was riding in a cart full of a weeks' worth of fire wood, two rabbits, a third one traded for the use of the wagon, and of course the fresh greens and roots.

 The cook looked up in time to see the boy stacking an arm load of fire wood.

"Where the hell you been boy, you been gone all day I thought you run off, whaaat the…?" The view of the load shut Cookie up.

 Masso continued unloading even before the Sergeant got to the full story and what he had brought in for his day's work.

"This is just a tip of the food tree out there Cookie. I can't believe no one has hunted there before. I suggest you let me work at night so no one will copy us."

So his life was not much different than at Dell Rosa. Masso still worked the fire, all the hauling, toting, peeling, boiling, and cleaning during the day. Then left after dark, Masso would work the woods for fresh food. With time, Masso would travel further out even being gone a couple days at a time, also doing reconnaissance about the area's assets.

When the officers began eating better, how or why was never asked but they suddenly found all the officers wanted to be fed only by them. Cookie now had new status among his peers from all the different companies. The old sergeant had now taken top position from Big Albert, who had been the top hog. Alberto had been the only cook who fed the Officer corps, at least until now?

One early morning Big Albert caught Masso coming in from his nightly foraging.

"Where you going you little bastardo? You owe me and I'm claiming my rights. You're going to be my bitch now and for that honor, I'm going to let you suck my big Sardinian cock right here and now." Albert had grabbed Masso by the scruff of his shirt as he walked by. He lifted him off the ground like he was a sack of potatoes and was shaking him hard as he was yelling at him, with the words, "here and now." Big Albert threw him down on the ground at his feet, and then dropped his pants as he slapped the boy.

Masso crawled to his knees, looking up at this angry fat man and put a fast plan together. "Sure Sergent Cook man," with his left hand he reached up and pulled the old yellowing cock and saggy sack down firmly and with his free right hand he reaches down into his boot coming out, with a razor- sharp dirk , that easily sliced through the delicate skin and flesh.

Masso then quickly rolled backwards, as the blood rushed from the old cooks crouch. The whole act was done while the fat old cook was busy watching the people's faces and enjoying the clapping hands. Until like a cold icicle stabbed him in the testes, did the pain hit. Then, the old bully had to face the reality, he had been neutered. By then it was too late to do anything but try to grab the boy, but with his paints around his legs. Big Albert tripped and falls, finding himself face down in the dirt. He was able to look up in time to see his nemesis' assistant, toss his prizes into his own cook's fire. He watched as the little bastard walked away, not even looking back.

Masso now also knew no one else would try making those types of demands on him.

The cook was taken to the med tent but there was not much that could be done but cauterize the wound, he lost a lot of blood and spent the next two days screaming in and out of conciseness, until he died. The screaming along with the stench of burnt flesh that was to permeate the air for days, were awake up calls to reality, for all the troops around.

This was what war is really about. People died, people get crippled men scream and there is a distinct odor of dying of burning flesh, that stench. These experiences will stay in the noses and memories, of all these men forever. Now it's all part of all of our realities. Masso thought to himself as he returned to his own camp- site.

"You are being charged with attacking and maiming a fellow solder, which in the end resulted in his death. These boards of officers are here today to decide your fate. We will determine the facts. Then this Military Tribune will determined if you are guilty or innocent and if you live or die for your actions. Do you understand soldier?"

"I do sir", replied Masso slowly, "but what I don't understand, is what are the charges? There is no written military code in any army I have known throughout history sirs that allows one solder to be forced to submit to another for an unwanted sexual assault by a senior soldier. Especially a superior ranking one, is this not true? I was solicited to fight the enemies of the Sardinian army, and I am prepared to give my limbs or life for the cause. But I do have the right to defend myself against all who would cause me harm just for their pleasure and sirs I will continue to do so." His words hung in the air, and no one spoke. "If that's all sirs' I have your dinner to prepare, a grouse n turnip stew I believe." Masso saluted and walked out before anyone had time to say anything.

The discussion after he left was short.

The youngest officer spoke first. "We need to make an example of this man. We can't allow this type of behavior to spread."

 Then one of the senior officers spoke, "He is right, he does have a right to protect himself. We all know it had been a practice in the past for men without women around to engage in homosexual exchanges, mem being men, but there were written rules that dealt with officers and their subordinates, acceptable behavior."

"Besides, the old cooks dead and this boy has been feeding us well since he joined up," said the General's aid.

 The junior officer who wanted his head was a Captain Arturo La Barba, his regiment's commanding officer and the nephew of Masso's Don. The final vote was three against one.

Life settled into a basic pattern for Masso. The regiment had a quarter master-corps, which had the basics for the cooks to draw off from to feed there men. Lots of corn meal, which was served in bread or as morning gruel, and of course pasta were the basics on the daily menu. Vegetables were added when available from area farmers. On a rare occasion a bit of meat or fowl parts would be added to those left overs if any from the previous meal. His nightly forages to the countryside were now not an unusual event and the centuries knew him by sight. His scavenging brought a larger variety of foods into the camp. Masso had been an expert at bartering with people no matter where he was since he was a child so now within a few months he knew where to go with in two days out, for many things like fresh bread and wine, cheeses, olive oil and melons.

Each morning Masso started at the desk of Corporal Rizzo , a shrewd, short and wirily man who was in his early twenty's. He ran the place like everything belonged to him. You had to sell him on giving you any little thing you needed.

On the second trip to the quartermaster's tent, Masso found a new approach in dealing with Corporal Rizzo.

"Sergeant I found this hive the other day and thought you might have some uses for some of its contents."

"It is Corporal Rizzo to you, and what is in here?

"Just some honey to sweeten your disposition a little, Corporal Rizzo."

"Ok Masso what do you need?" So from the start they had a working relationship. The corporal provided the basic items for trade, and Masso would come back with the bounty an always something extra for his partner.

Most of the new recruits trained and toughened up by marching for hours, then practice face- to -face one- -one combat with each other using unloaded rifles. Actually practicing to fire these weapons was few and rare. By the end of basic training they were to be ready to go to combat.

The cooks and helpers were not trained for anything but feeding. Masso had a plan to change that and with the insight of Corporal Rizzo he put together a small group of men from the cook's helpers' brigades. They were men that Rizzo had suggested might have what it would take to become traders like him-self. Masso had been swapping old stale surplus supplies that they were given to the quarter masters to feed their troops. Items of excess most wanted were corn meal, rice, and dry pepper. Masso in return got fresh produce and fruit, cheese, butter and baked goods. An occasionally a pig might be enticed to follow him down the road and those times, meat was served.

"Masso I have a few men I think will fit your bill. Private Divain, he has been a bit of a hot head and lost a give me job to an officer, as his sectary. It seems Divain is an educated man whose bad luck put him on the bottom of a long list of males in his father's line. So with little opportunities in the real world left, the only thing left for him was the Navy or the Army. He is trainable. Second is a duo of sorts. Charlie ...well he is a pretty boy with a growing ego and sharp wit. Then there is his muscle Gerome.... Dumb as a rock but devoted to Charlie. He works like two men and is as strong as three."

Just before the weekend the group met in the supply tent after the evening meal had been served and the evening work had been done. "You three have been asked here for an opportunity to get out from behind cooking pots and to gain a bit of independence, to be traders and hunters," Masso started his pitch.

"I did not join the army to be some dandy's writer of love letters, or a pasta boiler, and damn sure don't want to be a traveling merchant, I joined to fight and,"... A swishing sound was heard while Divain was stopped midsentence, as Masso's wooden staff's end whishing past Divian's nose missing it by hairs.

"If you will let me finish," the group all stood with full attention now only on the boy in front of them. His deeds were well known by then and his skills with a wood shaft were all the proof they needed at this moment. "This opportunity will allow you unsupervised time, time to do your hunting, gathering, trading. It will also allow you to be trained as warriors. Not just marching soldiers but real warriors. I am looking to form a small group of specially trained men to form a unit that will bring havoc to the enemy even before the big battles begin. Men who will be trained to, hit and run. We will be like bees we may not kill, but we sure can cause a lot of pain. Our actions will take attention off their plans. The job will not be easy nor will the lessons, that's a given. This is not for just any man. You have to be committed totally committed and fearless under pressure. **Finally,** my word is the last. You do as I say, the way I want it done, when I say it. If you cannot, then leave now. So who's in?"

"How is it that you, a just more than a boy yourself, hell you don't even have very much fuzz on your chin, know so much?" asked Charlie.

"I have been training for this my whole life, I grew up hunting for seeds, mushroom, plants that heal and roots that kill. My first weapon was my slingshot, and I can cripple or kill almost anything up to and including a full size man. My Patron made sure I was trained in all types of weapons and I can use accurately an artillery piece better than most seasoned soldiers. I have studies military campaigns and know many times even before the officers what to expect from there campaign and strategies. I maybe young, but I've been tested in combat, and you all know by now that even an old hairy cook does not stand a chance against me."

The group all laughed knowing the story, so they all stayed including Corporal Rizzo.

"It may take a few days to get you released from cooks' squadron and into the quarter masters corps, but we will start then." Masso was pleased with the first meeting.

"Masso, I want in", said Rizzo after the other three left, "I want to be a trainee too. "

"Glad you're in, and I am sure you will not regret it."

It is amazing what keeping fresh foods available to feed senior officers will do. Just by adding a fresh chunk of cheese or jar of wild honey from time to time and an enlisted man could get almost anything he wanted from an officer. Like an extra strip for now Sergeant Alberto Rizzo and a single one for his new assist, now Private Tomasso Del la Rosa.

Two days later the group met to beginning lessons on trading and of war.

"Your skills with people and being observant will be the most important tools to your success on the road. Also against any enemy you may face in a battlefield. Each, you approach with caution but without fear. Learn to watch the eyes, for their body will follow the eyes most of the time. Say your journey for the day takes you by a small dwelling hidden in in the woods. Always be aware of your total surroundings before you move forward. Now on the way to the dwelling's door, you find yourself facing a pack of hungry looking canines coming out from under the house and are looking to eat your ass up. Before you can make it to the dwelling's front door or even back to the cart you are lunch. Luckily, you have bits of fresh rabbit's feet in your pouch, to throw out so you can make it to your goal. Which in this case was a basket full of fresh turnips in exchange for a little corn flour. In battle you need to know if you're fighting on dry land or blood-soaked grounds, or maybe it will be over and on top of wounded or dead bodies. All this must be considered, and you must adjust you battle plan on the move, and still watch for addition hazards or other men who wish to get in your way. All of this must be dealt with even before the next confutation can be started."

Masso continues, "The dogs no longer being the issue, you must now put the lady of the house at ease even before offers and terms can begin. Observe everything about her. If she is toothless then hard tack would not be a good trade for her, but cheap corn flour is something she would have much greater need of."

"Watch as your enemy approaches you. Does he favor one side of his gait when walking or running? Is one arm lying lower than the other, showing exertion? Know what armament he is using, a rifle with bayonet or is he with sword? Know his weakness, spot it, and figure out your defensive plan and how to go for that weakest point. Like with the dogs, subversion, confusion, and surprise are your best weapons next to your skills as a warrior thinking on your feet and being willing to wound and kill. An as always, watch the man's eyes. Each exercise each training class will included basics combat skills and basic training in how to deal with every day people I have little tricks to teach you once you all are ready to move on to the next part of your training." Each of Masso's classes had lessons on situations they might encounter in either as a trader or as a solder. These exercises were meant to help them think fast on their feet so they could see several options to deal with the circumstance that was in front of them.

Thus began what was to be a nearly a year- long training program of physical and mental fitness. Masso set up physical work for them all to help with strength and balance. Also it would help them with their bodies' endurance. Skills with the staff were developed for aggression and defense. When swords were being taught, the first emphasis stressed was on defensive skills knowing the finer points strategy and position. His aim was for them to survive long enough and to be able to get so close. Then they could a use a knife or free hand aggressively against the opponent's eyes, nose, throat, or neck, all of which would cause the most damage with the least amount of effort when done right, and were rarely expected.

"Masso, what are your plans for Pretty Boy and his Ox, to continue working as a team?" Asked Rizzo early one morning after a particularly hard and strenuous hand-to-hand combat exercise.

"Actually as you probably noticed, Gerome is my biggest success. He listens well and executes precisely. I have had very little need to adjust him very much. Even with his greater size and your advantage of speed, he gives you the best defense and offence work out yet with staffs and with the bayonetted rifles. He has a quick mind too. He may be the real brains between those two. If we can get him to overcome his shyness I will send him out alone. I will need your help along with Divan's, to start giving him good feedback. No more Ox, it is Gerome from now on."

Masso also taught the group some basic plant and insect information. "A brew of certain easily identifiable plants can cure some ills, but the same plants also can kill or make you deadly sick if you know how to use them. Sick soldiers don't fight well if at…," was all they heard for months. "Watch for this plant or watch for this berry which will be blooming now."

"The other things I want you to be looking for will be little crawly weapons, like scorpions, or flying pest like hornets or bee's anything that stings, bites or just makes life unpleasant. Especially say when released in the camp's ammunition tent or food storage areas. These pests can do some of our work for us."

The group went out daily to the countryside trading for fresh bread, in- season vegetables, mushrooms, nut's, fruits, and honey were gathered by each waggoneer. Each man was to also to provide, as best as they could, wild game. The skills were given individually to fit the skill set of each man and to hone weaknesses.

It was an early crisp fall Sunday morning when Sergeant Albert Rizzo returned victorious from his first solo hunt. He returned bloody, a laceration on his right leg. His left hand was messy but not serious most of the blood being that of his prey. "Well," he began, holding each of the crew's attention before going on. "I was on my hands and knees, picking mushrooms when the beast first caught my attention. He snorted and grunted at me. He then started dragging his foot like a bull against the ground. Then, the next thing I knew, he is charging towards me with no provocation. I was lucky to have gotten my staff end up just in time to stick it partway in his throat. I don't know where it came from, but suddenly my right hand was holding my knife and I'm stabbing and cutting at his body. That mean ass angry boar was swinging his head trying to pull my staff out of his mouth. I guess he caught the side of my leg with his tusk, but he just grazed it. I had my left hand on his tusk trying to hold on, and they are a lot sharper than they look. In the end and in today's battle of life and death, I Sergeant Albert Rizzo was the luck victor, and tomorrow he will be our dinner." Upon which the story ended and Rizzo proudly took two steps and then fainted.

They contested and pushed each other so in the end they would fear nothing, including death itself. For, "The Cause," was the ultimate goal he had set for his group to learn, so as to be second nature when any type of combat they were to come upon." You will find that this training will allow our inside to control both mind and body without thought. Yes, you must know no difference inside no matter what is going on the outside no matter if it's hot and dry or wet or freezing outside." These were Masso's final words for that day, except "You all are doing well enough for the next phase. Tomorrow we move into the strategy sessions and how we will use field artillery accurately and effectively even with a small cannon."

It took a lot of trading to get the use of the company's signal cannon a smaller Napoleon 26" barrel with an inch and half bore.

"Where did you find baby cannon? It's so cute." Charlie wised off as the group met up miles from camp.

"She is just a much smaller version of her big brother that the Artillery corps has been training with. The principals though will be the same and in the hands of an expert can be very effective." So the basics of the math were explained several times. Again then again over the next months in several different ways until the principals were connected to the actions, which were to equate to the end results, hitting what you're aiming at, to produce the greatest destruction. The smaller bore meant smaller projectiles. To be effective the guys worked hard as a team.

One of the item that has always been in demand was explosives, for the ancient mining industries on the island. They have been active since the beginning of milieu and some area mines were still busy pulling out lead. Other areas were mining iron ore, copper, and silver. The big operations had a steady supply, but the smaller operations were always looking for dynamite or black power if dynamite was not available. This in-demand commodity, which the army had plentiful supply of, which could be traded, for many things including hard coins of silver. In his investigation of the island's resources Masso discovered this truth.

"Serge, what do you think the army is paying for lead these days?"

"Why do you ask?" He replied, "Oh I see, and what do we have here? I won't ask where you got this lead, or how, but I'll make some inquires. This looks a good enough that all the armament corps would need to do is adding heat and pore it directly into the molds. How much can we get of this?" Rizzo now asked, his attention perked?

"I can buy lead like this sample cheap. We'll buy it by the ton for only few pounds of black power, so make your inquires. I also saw a 33", cannon with a bore almost 5". It only weighs 125 pounds, and it can be very deadly. I think we can get it with a little silver traded to have someone to look the other away." Masso always had his eyes open, looking to put a deal together.

So the years went by with the tight group of traders and fighters continuing to fine tuning their skills. Masso was also always on the look out to acquire the finest private array of armaments, just for their own groups use, getting everyone ready for that day when all the training was to be put to the ultimate test.

New Year 1859

 Just weeks after the New Year's celebrations, a real reason for a celebration occurred. "Well my little group of terror fighters. I have got news that we all have been hoping for. The Minister of Piedmont Sardinia, Count Cavour, has signed an agreement of mutual defense with France's Napoleon the Third. Now for real the war for our independences has started. The Emperor Franz

Josef first and his Austrian empire will now have a real fight on their hands. His army's gotten fat and lazy. All we need now is to take what we want. With the French all in now, we can do that." Like a child receiving the perfect birthday gift Masso was truly happy. "Tonight we celebrate to what I hope is a started and then a very swift finish."

May 3, 1859 was the actual day Napoleon the Third declared war on the Austrian Empire, to which four days later the Austrian army moved onto Piedmont [*Turin*].

Masso called his group together one night before dinner. "The war has begun but it will be weeks before our military will be called to cross into the main land, to fight. The French are thirsting for blood and already heading to Montebello. I got Captain La Barba to sign off on our leaving now. We have been assigned as advance surveillance. Unofficially we are havoc raisers. We are to do any and everything possible to make as many of the Austrian troops lives, as miserable as possible, so we can soften them up even before our own troops face them. This is what we have been training for, men. Tomorrows 300 nautical miles will likely be rough, so don't eat much tonight I'll have a brew for us in the morning to help with the sea heaves." These were the instructions given them by Masso the night before they left.

So in the early morning hours the small, well-trained group of men left, with little in the way of provisions except for one sack with the 33" bronze cannon that Gerome was carrying. The five left out of the port of *Bastia* in an old single sail trading skiff. The arrival to the small port city of *Vado Ligure* just south of *Genoa* went unnoticed and the men pale but still in good enough condition to quickly moved out of town towards Torino. The units' first stop was just a few miles up the road to *Carlo Mintenotte* to gather as much Intel about troop movements of both sides and a pick up few provisions that they would be needed before the first plan was to be executed.

The group had not meant to drawn attention, but an alert Austrian captain noticed how they seemed to flow as a group and became suspicious. He gathered twelve of his men and followed the group at a distance. Masso and his men were just outside of town, eating dinner, when the captains group began firing at them, pinning them down as the sun set. Soon in the darkness the men saw three sets of fires surrounding them?

"At first light, they will attack us, so we must give them the unexpected. We will bring the battle to them tonight." Masso's orders were simple, "We have been practicing now it is time to execute." He broke them down into two- man units and sent them out, in black face. When their heads were down they became invisible. Masso sent them out to destroy all those who were at the fires, to test their skills. He would stay behind and fire the cannon at the officer's quarters now lite up by a lantern. "Timing is everything, so as soon as you hear the big gun roar, move in and destroy." The cannon's shot destroyed the canvas tent, and the officer sitting at his desk writing of his soon- to- be victory. Rizzo and Gerome were in the farthest camp as soon as the gun went off. They stepped out of the darkness, and easily shot the now four standing soldiers who had their dinner plates still in their hands. All they saw were white eyes, before effortlessly being dispatched. Divain and Charlie only found one man around his fire, who was quickly dispatched by Divain with a quick knife to his throat. Then out of the dark the three others came charging, rifle raised but too excited to hit anything, and were shot dead promptly. The cannon now was aimed at the last fire side, hitting the fire directly killing two and wounding a third man who was now a human torch, running and screaming at the top of his lungs, in his burning uniform. It was Charlie's shot from the darkness that put him out of misery.

From Torino they split up. Charlie, whose father was German, and had a working knowledge of the language went with   Masso and were now heading toward *Gallaratese* just north of *Milan*. Masso was hoping to intercept the northern invading Austrian army, now coming from Como. The other three of the group headed towards Italian General Garibaldi's forces that were heading to *Varese* to defend the town, and getting it ready for the upcoming combat.

Two days later the two- some were riding in a single axel old cart which was being pulled by an old stoop back mare. Her load was two casks of brandy and fresh bread, butter, and sausages. The young men now dressed as area farm boys who were looking to sell for silver these needed supplies to the invading Austrian Army of General Karl Von Urban.

When the two came upon the troops just outside *Saronno*, they were directed to the back, where the supply post had been recently been set up that morning.

Even though the quartermaster was busy, he stopped and came forward when the cart pulled up.

"What have we here?" the half dressed, sweaty sergeant asked as he approached the two young men.

Charlie jumped down and spoke in German, "My brother and I are here to see if the great Austrian Army might have a need for a cask or two of this fine ancient brandy, or maybe some fresh bread and the butter you might have a need for? We also have some fine summer sausages; can you use any of these items?"

"How much for the brandy and where is it from?" Asked the sergeant.

"We don't take any paper notes, only silver, but if you take all of it, he looks up. Masso , looked down and shrugged his shoulders, while looking back over this companions head. Coming up on a beautiful white stallion was the most pompous looking man Masso had ever seen, all dressed up in a high ranking officer's uniform? He had a clean- shaven face except for a wild mustache under his nose and his hair on the sides of his head was swept forward, so to appear to be horns. The hat on his head looked as if it was about to pop off.

"Excellent my provisions have arrived. Unload them at my tent sergeant at once."

"No sir, these are our goods, and we are here to offer a sale." Charlie quickly spoke up, "We are just working out payments."

"No payment due here, you need to support our troops boys. We are only here to protect you from those who would deny you your freedom which the great Austrian Empire affords you. No our thanks are your payments."

When the sergeant tried to mount the cart he found Masso's foot in his gut pushing him back. What Masso did not expect was the officer's riding crop which he used quickly on the boy.

For the most part most of the tassels on the end missed their mark, but three did hit his face below his left eye cutting with the razor tip ends and leaving three parallel deep to the bone gashes on his face.

The sergeant pulled Masso off the cart throwing him down on the ground and climbed over him as he mounted the cart then with a smirk began pulling away. Masso got to his feet, running to get to the cart to retrieve his backpack and staff before they too were part of the plunder. Two soldiers stepped into the roadway and tried to stop him from leaving, yelling some nasty sounding word's, **"Halt, Jetzt den Beutel ubergeben."** Blood was now pouring from his three line wounds on Masso's face giving him a weakened appearance. The two Austrian soldiers approached with swagger, and when the first one reached out for the bag he got a broken nose instead as Masso drove his right hand's heel deep into the large nose of the solider. All around could hear the cartilage crunching as it collapsed inward. The first swish the second man heard was just before the large end of the staff meets his kneecap.

The sight of blood pouring out of his fierce face and the skill with the staff was enough for the remainder of the observers hanging around to turn and let the two leave without further harassment.

The first surprise they had left for these officers was the hornets' nest attached to the bottom of the cart to make it look like it had been there for a long time. The nests exit hole covered by a small plug of wood. So when one of the barrels was unloaded and the small plug pieces pushed out of place, the hole was exposed. The now the very mad as hell hornets came out angrily looking for blood. The two waited just close enough and long enough to hear the invasion and the screams.

Laughing lightly as they walked away Charlie's response was, "Well that didn't end as you expected did it Boss?

"Actually except for the officer part it went perfectly. By tonight most of the officers who share the booty will find themselves poisoned. They don't know it yet but when it does take hold it will be a sickness like nothing they have ever felt before. They will not be thinking of battle when they are wishing for death themselves. The brew takes a few doses and time to build up so they will never think it's the brandy or the sausages. It will not show up today but when the battle begins, soon I think, it will be too late."

They stopped only long enough to treat Masso's face, using small barbed Botar thorns as clamps. Charlie with Masso's directions pushed the thorn through the two sides of each of the cuts pulling them back together, the next on pushing down in the opposite direction going back and forth until all three gashes were treated and then coated with honey as an antiseptic.

"Well Masso, it will just have to do. Even if I say myself, you now got the face that only a lonely, horny and old woman would want." Charlie the forever joker says of his work with that boyish grin in his eye. "Where we off to now Boss?"

"We will head toward *Varese*. That's where I think Garibaldi and his 7000 troops will be gathering for the defense of the town. It has what looks to be the best place to fight. Our troops' having the higher grounds, gives the advantage to Garibaldi. I think the two armies' next real engagements will be there."

On May 26th General Karl Von Urban and his better equipped and under normal circumstances larger army mounted the first attack. He was met with heavy resistance. The other three of the group following the plan, found themselves in position to best help disturbed the enemy where they least expected. High on the hills besides the Austrian army they set up the cannon shooting down at the Austrians fixed artillery positions. The plan was simple, one or two shots then on to another artillery position. Masso's idea was with one small cannon being shot by experts, it could be very effective in destroying one of the enemies' most important strengths and before they could react. The threesome would have moved on before they were located.

 In the critical part of the battle that day, their brandy treated regiment was called up to be the greatly needed help. Those reinforcements were now too sick a group of men, to show up. They no longer had any officers who were physically able to make it to the field of combat that day or the next.

Masso and Charlie got in town in time to watch the battle from high in one of the many steeples that the city is famous for. "Look way over to their right flank. No, Divain higher, you need to, yes a direct hit, do you see that, Charlie, ooh, that one was perfect."Masso was leading with cheers.

"Oh my sweet Jesus, that one just hit the artillery piece directly. You could not ask for anything better of them, Masso. I wish I was there." Charlie was getting more excited with each shot.

They watched as their comrades shot and destroyed one artillery units after another. Garibaldi's troops held up against these seasoned Austrians, and never gave an inch. With no back up troops Urban had no other choice but to withdraw back to Como, tail between his legs.

"Tonight Charlie, I want you to follow Urban's troops. They will retreat and somewhere around *Gallarate* put yourself there and find out who's the Austrian's agent there. Try to sell him this fake communication from Garibaldi to General Garrzo." Masso explained to Charlie. "I don't think our general is ready to face Urban quit yet. What he will do is fake coming for the Austrian's head on. Instead Garibaldi I believe will go north to the lightly defended *San Fermo* pass. It's a smarter move and it will put him again, in the superior position. Our troops then only have to defend the pass. All a defending army has to do to win is survive, and in the end, it's the survivors who win the war, right?"

By May 27^{th,} Urban got fresh reinforcements from Austria, and was again ready for battle. His newest intelligence told him the Sardinian Army was on the move and on its way, inforce, to do battle outside Como on the plains.

By the time Herr General realized what had happened and his information was false. The Sardinia army was victorious and was now totally in control of the critical pass where the Austrian's reinforcements, and supplies' had to come through.

General Urban's troops when they did finally get to *San Fermoy* pass were repeatedly pushed back. Then with nothing left to try he and his army fled back first to Como. Then back to Milan leaving behind all their supplies in Como.

Back in Como the five met back up. Their new assignment was to over- see the huge surplus supplies the Austrian's abandoned, and direct the supplies to Sardinia troops as needed.

"Masso, what is that on the cheek of your face? What happened to you two?" Rizzo asked at the group's first meeting.

"I was looking at the wrong set of eyes," Masso replied, "and I lost focus of the real threat. I had to learn from that mistake, the hard way." The boy admitted, "But Charlie and I executed our part of the plan and, we were, quite glad to see your three's success in execution of your objectives. You guys took out three of their strongest artillery pieces, and disrupted the other four on their flank. I could see them lose focus after each of our cannon hit their target and then their artillery men kept looking around worried if they would be next. Your pinpoint successes were enough to weaken the right side of the battle field allowing the French to push right through. All in all it was us five who really won these battles, even if it will never be acknowledged. Now with that being said, we now have a choice. We could go without orders and head out towards Milan try to pick up the trail and continue harassing the Huns**… but**... I also see too good an opportunity to profit from our current situation. So I want to share an idea. This war is over. The tide is flowing for Napoleon the third and his Sardinian lackeys. Shortly the Austrians will settle.”

“You really think this is over?” Charlie asked, “I was just getting into this butt kicking.”

 “Yes I do, they will give up some areas in order to keep a bit more than they deserve. All this will be worked out before the first cold front. At the latest, then the papers will be signed. What will the army have need of us then? We will find ourselves unemployed, then what?   History tells us, old solders make poor employees, sailor’s maybe they still can sail but not combat ready solders. With that in mind, I think we work well as a team. Trust each other and importantly you all trust me. If you want, I think we can continue our work outside the war and use your same skills domestically. Sicily’s royalty is gone, and the big estates are owned by men who live in big cities on the mainland or in *Palermo*. Some are actually owned by the mother church. All the same they have no one to oversee their security from the bad elements of society. Men who have no scruple, men who engage in thievery and ransom, to make their livings. We can handle everything they are doing and be more effective for our clients. We have been trained for this, so why not sell our services?”

"Masso you are such a clever son of a bitch. You have been putting this whole thing together from the start haven't you? How do you come up with these ideas? You certainly have an old warrior's soul and the luck of that saint of yours riding on your shoulders." Rizzo said as he was still laughing after he expressed his revelations.

Over the next couple of hours the group ate, and tossed out ideas and many more questions were asked, until the one everyone wanted, was asked.

"How much is the pay and how soon do we start?" the question finally asked by Divain, always the group's pragmatists.

"The pay will be better than you're making now for sure, and there will be opportunities to become wealthy. Well what do you think? The question then, brings us back to the beginning point of this conversation. Our current opportunities. We can take a portion of these supplies and redistribute them to vendors with hard silver for ourselves. So we all share in the work and cash. After we divide the moneys it will be up to each of you to decide if you want to continue and join up or take your pile of lira and go and do as you wish when you are released. Since I don't see any objections let's start by counting what we have and how much. Then Rizzo and Gerome can go to *Geneva* with some of it. It is a port town so cash will be there and dealers who will gladly buy for the right price."

Not too greedy but with keen eyes Masso and Rizzo met that after noon to go over the list. "Pick out all the best sizes of boots, the largest blankets, and all the meal of oat flour. If they ask about the flour we can say we had to dump it because it had gotten wet and was no good. Also pull few tons of lead billets from the stack, they will not likely miss it," Masso told Rizzo.

"Ok but I think we should leave the gunpowder alone." Rizzo suggested. "The central command will know down the last grain how much is still here. Gerome and I also went through the mixed armaments and put aside the best rifles, bayonets, and the few handguns as well as several axes, but surprisingly Gerome found a good selection of well-crafted swords. If we're going to start this new venture, then we are going to need more than one artillery piece."

"Good thinking. Get the goods loaded and you two make sure you're ready to leave at dusk. You should try to work a deal with one of those Jewish merchants, down at the harbor. Find one who sells provisions to the boats that come in. They always have cash."

The five took enough of the supplies to make the risk profitable but not enough to be noticed. The rest of the surplus supplies were shipped out to the several different troop locations over the next four days.

June 4, the French and Sardinian army crossed the *Ticino* River and out flanked General Gyulan the Austrian's Supreme Command. The French army took them by surprise and caused another big defeat, this time in *Milan*. That same day the General resigned and the Emperor Franz Josef took control of the forces himself.

Franz Josef first reorganized his armies and withdrew them to the Minco River, at the border between *Lombardy* and *Venetia*. However, he did not plan to keep them there but instead launched a counterattack to try and retake *Lombardy*. The Austrian armies met the French and Sardinians at *Solferino*.

On June 24, 1859, in what would prove to be the war's decisive clash, the Austrians held their positions all day, but faced difficulties as they were split into three forces, the Centre being at Solferino while two other units fought to the north and south, at San *Martino* and *Medole* respectively. The Sardinian troops at *San Martino* fought all day despite being outnumbered, and prevented their Austrian opponents from being able to support their comrades at *Solferino*. The Austrian positions were finally captured at around 8pm. Only a couple of hours earlier, French reserve troops had finally broken through in the center of the battlefield at Solferino itself. The Austrians in the south at *Medole* had also been forced to retreat after a day's hard fighting. Franz Josef's armies withdrew to their quadrilateral fortresses at *Verona, Peschiera, Legnago* and *Mantua*.

The two emperors involved, Franz Josef and Napoleon III, were both concerned about the scale of the losses and how they might affect their popularity and prestige in their home countries. They decided to meet to discuss a peace treaty. Controversially, they failed to include the Sardinians in the talks. It was agreed that Lombardy would be ceded to France, who would then pass it straight on to Sardinia. Venetia would remain in Austrian hands, and Sardinia would give Savoy and Nice to France. It was intended that the pre-war rulers of the other Italian states would be restored, partly to stop Piedmont-Sardinia becoming too powerful by taking control of the smaller states. These terms were all made official in the Peace of *Villafranca*, signed on July 11, 1859. When the treaty was made public, Chief Minister Cavour of *Sardinia* resigned in protest over the terms and the lack of *Sardinian* inclusion.

The take on the group's first joint venture was one thousand lira worth of silver and gold pieces.

"I have never seen that much money in all my life," said Gerome. "And truthfully, I have no idea what to do with mine."

"Well, I know exactly what I am going to do. Live it up at the fanciest whore- house I can find and," was all Charlie got out before Masso broke them out of their fantasy exchanges.

"Two hundred lira can buy each of you, a new life. A house, a business, a herd of sheep or cows, and a coral full of horses. This money can be your independence. Or you can piss it off, like it seems our rooster here wants to do. So your choices are simple, do you buy a hen and feed off her eggs every day or just eat her now! No matter what you chose put some of it away for the future, because if I know one thing for sure, it will be here sooner than later." With that he sat down with Rizzo and counted out the cash, giving each man, his stack of coins.

By the end of July, Rizzo and company were given a new assignment to take his men and search the country sides for deserters from both sides and to confiscate any weaponry that they were to come across.

Gerome and Charlie were working the area closets to the camp waiting for their discharge papers, due in any day. The whole chemistry of the group had changed. The lira now made them all equals.

The group still met in the mornings to share bread and cheese, whenever possible.

Divain cornered Masso early one morning before breakfast. "Masso , I am in with your plan, if you say we can make serious wealth I believe in you. All I got to know do you believe in me?"

"Why all of a sudden such a question my friend, what's going on with you?"

"I wrote my family or really my mother, to let her know I was alright and due to be discharged soon probably very soon. I sent it a few weeks back. I did not go into any detail, but I let her know I had been in combat and faced the enemy and defeated him. Any way yesterday I got a letter back, but it was not from my mother but my father. *Congratulations on your promotion from being a glorified secretary to a real soldier. May you career choice bring you much joy and happiness. We are all doing very well, and your brother John is exceeding all our expectations as the new president of the business, etc.....* lots of how rich and well the whole family and extended family was doing. He would have shit himself if he knew I had been a cook's assistant. Anyway, I have no future back there, and if you think I can fit into your plans, then count me in. I am here to do whatever you need me to do."

Masso reached out and with both hands grasped his new partner's arm. "Divain, you know most of my own story, my family is the land. It gives me all I need. We are brothers and I would have never brought you in if I did not believe in you. So I am most certain it will not be a poor choice when you look back years from now my brother."

As they sat around the morning feast of bacon, cheese and bread they came back to the same game, what to do with the liras.

"You know Charlie and I were outside of Como the other day, out by the lake." Gerome tells the group of their previous day's adventures. "We came upon a beautiful chalet lodge and went in for a coffee. The views were so breathe taking, the air so clean. I have never been so drawn in to one place as I was there. Anyway, I got into a conversation with the owner. He says his business is busy only 7 to 8 months a year, the winters are cold with very little business, or visitors except for Christmas time. His wife is ill, and he had to move her into Genova with its milder climate. Now he is thinking about selling out. So we talked it over he gave me the numbers he had done the last seven years. It is growing better every year, repeats and new clients. I gave him a down payment so I guess I have a home base. Don't worry though. I already got someone to run the day today, while were out making Sicily a safer place." Now with Gerome on board, Masso had three of the four for the new organization, the **Alliance or Our Thing.**

One early fall morning Masso confronted his sergeant. " Say Rizzo , hop on board you need to get out of that tent and enjoy the beauty of the day and ride the road with me, what do you think?"

"I got so much to do, but…. what the fuck, yeah sure, let's go. I need to get back in the field. So where we heading this morning, corporal Del La Rosa?"

"The town of *Sondrio* is north east of here and since ancient times it has been famous for two things, do you know for what?"

"No, what?" Rizzo shrugged.

 "The town started as an ancient Roman military post for one, built here to cover the real reason for the town. It is a strategic pass. This one goes through the Alps, directly into Austria. If anyone wants to slip into or more importantly out of this country without being noticed, this is the best route. So that's where were going."

The two travel past vineyards that had been producing for centuries, and hilled areas that were scattered with old broken down stone structures long abandoned by the owners for better opportunities elsewhere.

"Let's cross over into Austria and then work our way back," Rizzo suggested.

It was as they were coming back from the last stop in Austria looking down at the winding steep road below, that luck was to shine on them. They had stopped beside the top of the road before going back down to share a bit of fresh bread and cheese. Walking around, just taking the beauty of the location, Rizzo happened to look down over the side.

"Masso, look at what we have coming our way. It looks like we may have found something worth checking out, what do you think?" The sight was being viewed by both men now. "Though I can't see his face, that horse I would know anywhere. I believe it was her rider, an Austrian General, who gave me these three, scars on my face. What do you think he's got in that covered wagon?" Seconds tick by as the two just stood and watched the two person caravan moving slowly up the road, far below, towards them.

"I bet you can't knock the fancy hat off the rider from here with that sling shot of yours, what do you think?" Rizzo said jokingly.

"A silver coin, on it you say?" Masso replied as he reached down for the perfect shape and weigh stone. His sling shot now loaded began its slow wind up. Each whirl, building and building speed with each circular revolution.

Far below, the rider stopped to say something to the driver of the wagon, and as he does, he turned the horse around for just a moment. With a, what do I have to loose attitude, moment,

Masso sent his stone not down toward the target but upward creating an arch approach as one would with an artillery piece.

Something, a sound or reflective light drew the rider's attention. Pulling the horse back around as he looked up, screening his eyes with one of his hands to block out the sunlight for a better view. Within seconds three things happened almost instantly.

First, the two men's eyes locked with instant recognition by both men. Second, the rider's movement changed the location of where the stone was to land, not on the officer's head as planned. The projectile did hit though with great force the white stallion's rump, grazing his hide. The third action was when horse's rear feet jumped up off the ground in unison and kicked backwards, thus hitting square in the head the draft horse pulling the wagon, killing it instantly. One other action was created or expected. When the rear feet of the horse came off the ground it caused the animals front feet to take most of the horse's weight pushing the horses head down, also propelling the man over the wounded animals head and shooting the rider upside down over the mountain roads edge. Stopping only after he hit an old ravaged tree. His body now was impaled on a broken branch upside down, arms stretched out over his head. His two legs folded back over each side if the tree's trunk, as if he was now was riding the tree upside down, to hell.

"Damn, I know nothing you are going to say will make me believe you had planned that. No sir. By the way, you owe me a silver coin." Rizzo spoke as they came down the road in their own horse drawn cart toward the scene of the action.

"He is not wearing his hat now is he? And that was the bet." Silently they rode for a while, each man deep in his own thoughts. "Never in my deepest dreams would I have ever thought I'd ever meet up with that pompous ass again, but it seems our fate was to meet one more time, with me being the one providing the surprised actions, first this time." Masso was thinking out loud to himself.

That shot, one in a million. How did he know? Why not thrown the rock just down directly? No he has to do it artfully. His instincts are so honed. He was already reacting before most people are acting surprised. This man, in whose hands, I have put my future? These were Rizzo's private thoughts coming down the road?

"Masso, this is a magnificent horse probably one hundred percent pure Arabian. I have seen at horse sales, animals not even this beautiful go for thousands of Lira." Razzo gingerly jumped down from the cart walking slowly and peacefully up to the visibly spooked animal. He bent over and whispered something into the horse's ear. Masso could hear but a word here and there. The words were though, of a strange language. "His right hindquarter seems bruised and has some swelling. He is not going to be pulling any wagon but he can walk on it. Nothings broken that I can tell."

The two slowly approached the cloth covered wagon, not knowing what happened to the driver or if he was even still around. If so, was he armed? What they found though was a wagon with one of its rear wood spoked wheel hanging over the side of the road with nothing but free air under it and with the left rear wheel close to the edge. The whole rear end of the wagon was on the verge of falling over the edge of the mountainside. The only thing holding it in place was the leather and wood that was strapped to the dead horse and its bulk weight.

"Unless the driver is inside, I think he ran as fast as he could after his wagon stopped its backward movement and you're raining stones from above stopped falling. Let's chock these wheels before one of us climbs on board." Razzo put one big stone in the back of the wheel and one on the back side of the two left wheels, while Masso put a few around the front right one.

Like two excited kids on their birthday the contents of the wagon drew both of them to jump up on the seat together. "Hurry up untie your side," Rizzo barked orders like the sergeant he was.

"Say Rizzo, what did you whisper to the horse to quite him down?" Masso deliberately toying with his mate as he slowly untied the ropes holding down the canvas top.

"It was just an old Jewish prayer my father use to use on his horses, it seems to work. Oh sweet Mother Mary, would you look at all this treasure. This guy must be the best thief to have ever lived." Rizzo's eyes were now lite up.

"It looks like he was going to take his spoils of war home even if his side lost. These paintings are old masters I have seen that one in one of Don Leonardo's art books. All these silver items come from churches and from large estates they ransacked. See those bolts of cloths, Rizzo; they had to been imported all the way from Asia. It's called silk and women will kill for it I'm told. It seems our General here had the first choice of the spoils for sure. The quick look around let them know they had hit a gold mine but Masso hand hit a hollow sound as he was climbing down.

"Do you hear that Masso?" Rizzo asked as the two both heard the galloping feet of horses coming up the canyon walls. Where Rizzo was the sergeant, they both knew in reality his corporal was the best man to create a working plan.

"Take a couple rifles and find yourself a good view and defensive position up there in the trees, you'll know when and if I you need to step in."

Masso turned back to the wagon and found the seat was also a lid for a concealed storage, and as he lifted it he saw inside a new chrome revolver with white horn handles, in a simple leather holster, sitting on top of neatly stacks of silver bullion. He quickly pulled the revolver out and promptly shut the lid, putting the cash out of his mind and focusing on the coming horses first.

Masso was busy applying a mud and herb plaster on the wounded horses' bruised muscles when the thundering group of horse men came upon the site. Masso whose back was turned away from the new arrivals, ignored them like he was expecting them to continue on.

"We are here to get the horse and wagon so back away boy."

Masso ignored the voice and just kept on rubbing the horses flank as the group of what he estimated to be between five and six riders in all looked on.

"I'm talking to you boy. Leave my horse alone."

"My name, you lying piece of shit, is Corporal Del-La-Rosa" Masso spits out as he turns around and now faces the leader. "This wounded horse belongs to the Sardinian army. If you want to speak to me again you can call me Corporal Del-la-Rosa, or just keep your tongue silent.

"The driver of this wagon is a citizen of our town and put his life at risk to serve this wagon and her load, fighting barrages of stones barely coming out with is life. You see the poor dead horse and the badly wounded one you're treating. Look at that poor

Austrian. What did he do but travel this road to his home. Which as I said, was Gizmo's job, so we need to finish the contract, and..."

"Your man, Gizmo was it? Well your Gizmo ran away after only one stone was thrown, by me by the way. That elegant dressed gentleman, that someone in your village has been hiding, was an Austrian General. He was a wanted man. Now it seems, he got what he deserved. As the ranking solder here of the Sardinian Army, I will confiscate his property as is our right. So go home and thank your blessings I don't bring the whole division into your town and find out who was helping and hiding this enemy."

"One thing you missed, scar face, is you are one unarmed boy against seven armed men, so step aside or Otto there is going to put a hole in you." The man beside him raised his shotgun. Moments later the first shot Rizzo fired hit the shotgun holding fat man between his shoulders knocking him forward dead.

Masso pulled out his newest chrome tool and fired two shots. The first hit Gizmo. The second shot, the speaker who was now rushing forward with a saber raised. Rizzo's last shot hit the shoulder of one of the men in the back row. It was enough for the remaining to turn around and head back down the road the way they came.

"Nice shooting there, Sergeant, right on target and more importantly on time." Masso praised his partner.

"We are going to have to pull the dead horse's carcass away first before we can even begin thinking of pulling this wagon back on the road, so let's put more rocks behind these wheels before we unharness the dead animal," Rizzo suggested. They worked as a team to remove the leather harnesses and even then, they had to pull her out by her rear legs to do that. Now with the extra horses the dead men no longer needed, they pulled the loaded wagon out easily. They hooked up both wagons with fresh horses and each pulled behind their wagon two of the newfound horses. The men made it a point to pull through the town in the darkest part of the night to avoid any more confrontations.

The two's first stop was before they came close to their camp. "So how much do you think we have here, Masso? There is so much here, it's unbelievable. I don't know where or what to look at first." Rizzo was caught up in all the luxury and potential wealth. "That was the luckiest stone to have ever been thrown. Well except maybe David's but certainly the second best. Really Masso, how much do you think we got here? "

"Let me ask you something more important Rizzo, how much would you be willing to spend of it to buy your way out of your contract with the Army, walk away free to do as you want?"

"You think we could really do that? How much would it take to get that done?" The sergeant's attention now focused on what was to be said.

"Exactly, how much?" Masso answered back. "So let's find a spot to store the Arabian and that gray mare she's the best of the other three and the money wagon and we'll bring in two of the dead men's horses as bait. We will have to work our way up to the right someone who can make that happen for you, Divain, and my-self. It will take whatever it takes. Don't tell anyone about what happened until we are done and back in civilian clothes again. Yes you can pick an item or two for yourself now."

When the two got back Charlie whose enlistment was over, had gotten his release papers and left with lira burning his hands.

Gerome too was also about to leave to close the paper work on his lakeside lodge.

"Masso, Charlie said he would catch up with us later, and I'll be back next week. Then I will be ready to do whatever you need me to do for, **Our Thing."**

Later that night, after the officer's dinner of chicken and noodles with a rich cream sauce, Masso approached the well fed Captain La Barba. "Sir, might I have a moment of your time?"

With a quizzical look, "What do you need now Corporal?"

"Well sir as you probably know, there are men whose life in the military fit well, say like yourself sir. Then others like my-self and a few of my men, well sir we are not really made for the military life. You probably already know that, but we have a contract, and,..."

"Get to the point. You want to know what your future in the military will be. Well I'll tell you. Cutting potatoes, onions and making meals like tonight's, for the remainder of your long contracts is what I see in your futures. Does that answer your question? If so, I have a card game waiting for me," the captain answered briskly.

"Yes sir, but contracts can be renegotiated, changed for the betterment of both sides. That is, if both parties are in agreement, is it not so sir? So now hear me out. Say if someone wanted to buy their contract out and even add a bonus fee for the individual who was to make that's happen, that s possible is it not, sir?"

"I have never heard of any such thing. Besides, it would take a field commanders signature for that and you don't have enough money for one of you, let alone all three. Masso you would need a saddle bag full of lira to make all the people up the command happy enough to sign off. Even if it was possible for one man, for three, it's not happening."

"Yes sir I understand, but I have six silver coins here to bet that if we provide enough bacon to the right few men whose nod and acceptance of the deal could be made, even a few exceptions. The war is over, our Army does not need us, and I got more of these." Masso puts in Arturo's hand 6 silver coins, "this could be a sample of what could be coming your way, so what do you say Captain?"

"Where are you getting this much cash, and what are you really up to? If you want my help you need to be totally honest with me. I too have a lot on the line if I do this. It even may kill my own military career. But most importantly, am I releasing a curse on my own family?"

For a long moment the two locked eyes, each man trying to read the others sincerity. Masso knew his Captain was telling the truth and his concerns well founded.

"You have known of me, where I come from, but you don't know my heart and I do understand your concerns Captain. What you do know I am fearless. I will complete any given task even the ones that seem impossible. What you don't know is that Don Leonardo La Barba, my Patron, and you're Uncle. He had appointed me Abortrador of the family a day before he was attacked. Father Stefano was there as well. My intent is first to protect the family at all cost. That is why he appointed me, second to try to put the Don's dream of a United Citrus Union together." Masso was honest and laid his plan out to get the families estate back, to re- establish the orchard as a premium producer and lastly, increase the La Barba family's wealthy and power.

"And what is your plan for my father and my brothers in this scheme of yours?" Asked the captain? "We have been given the ass end of the families business for years. Getting by, while Frances and his uncles live like royalty and we have to clean up the mess they leave from poor choices, all the while running the La Barba and Luccus Trading Company."

"Your side of the family is still La Barba. My work is for the betterment of the whole family, your side included. No favorites, but to keep everyone up on events and be the judge and final decision maker, like the Don. I do take this responsibility honestly and will do whatever it takes, to get this job done, just as he would."

They talked well into the night, asking and answering each other's questions. In the end they agreed on a plan of action. Captain La Barbra would approach the right man in the right position, whose greed for power but more importantly greed for money made this plan work. The commanding officer's second in command, a colonel would make up the honorable discharged papers .The colonel would add the documents in with several other papers the commander had to sign for the day. That day, a white Arabian horse would be presented to the General. When the commander's attention was more likely to be focused on a beautiful horse and not on the few papers before him that were to be signed.   In the end the plan went smoothly, with the colonel's price resolved for five hundred a man. Funds were provided by the Alliance, as loans to each of the four members not already released, and were the new organization's first bit of business.

A week later the group met for the first time as an operating organization in the most beautiful lake and woods environment any one of them had been too. Even the air had a sweet clean smell, all the best of food, drink, and creature comforts that Gerome's Inn could provide.

"Gentlemen, and I use the term loosely, I wish to thank you all for allowing me to join your money making venture." Charlie was back, broke and partly sober.

"Thank you Charlie for your touching and to the point remarks." Masso was sitting on the side of the table not at the head but when he stood up to address his group. A sixteen year old war scarred veteran, knew he was their 'MAN', each for his own reason. "In life we must work to feed ourselves. Now if this work happens to bear excess then that's all the better. The odds are in our favor, and if my plans work then we all will find we all will have excess. Too excess and success," Masso raised his glass in a toast.

"Yea-ha". "Oh yes." "Great idea." "Who's going to arguing with that?" "You're the boss so yes, yes, yes." In that moment in time, each man putting it in his own words their commitment to, **Our Thing** the **Alliance** and to Masso leadership.

"Each of you has a special talent and the Alliance will use those skills. Rizzo I want you and Charlie to go to *Piazza Armerina* and find a building to buy. I want to open an inn with food and some friendly gambling in the back. Divain I want you and Gerome each to travel and trade. I want you to talk to the country people, and get a feel for what their concerns are about the new Government, and their concerns of their own safety. Also collect for me numbers of what and how many lemons, olives, grapes, and almonds the farms are harvesting. Find out who the big growers are and who the smaller growers sell their harvest to. Arturo will be going to *Palermo* to see after the Don and begin to make appearances in public as the new face of the La Barba family and the Alliance. He is a war hero, and a concerned nephew of a great Don returning. He will be our foot into politics and our back doors protection. I still have a few things to do, roads to build. One more thing, keep your eyes open for men that might fit into the organization, and lastly we will meet back in *Piazza* in two weeks."

The sun rose early over Lake Como, and Charlie was already waiting in ambush for Masso to return from his early, early walk he was so famous for. "Say boss, if I am going to help Rizzo set up the town's newest and finest establishment for gentlemen, well I need just a few liras till my first pay day, what you say?"

"Charlie you left with enough silver to live well for years and just weeks later you come asking for more?"

"Look boss it is not like you think, I went home first. Found my mom and sister, who now has two brats and no man, plus my youngest brother all living in one room, a space you would not want even those Huns to live in. My mom was supporting the family by working at a bakery for pence a day and a few loaves of very old and stale bread. I found them a store front property with a large living area on the second floor and a kitchen large enough to put in a second oven, so my family now runs their own bakery, and they have a way to take care of themselves. I bought a few pieces of clothing. I also spent a few days at a gaming house, at great personal expense I might add. I gambled to learn the secret of this one particular dice game. It took me two days of winning some and, losing more, to come up with their angle."

"Which is," asked Masso?

"First, odds are always in favor of the house, and second most importantly, they cheat. Did I mention I spent my own money?"

"Ok I still owe you some money Charlie. I figured you'd be back sooner than later so let's say I hedged your bets a bit. Anyway, here's 5 lira, for your pocket now."

With cash in their pockets provided by the Alliance, each man left that morning to begin their new lives. Arturo and Masso left on the pay load wagon still loaded with over three thousand pounds of silver under the seat and an interior still half full of war booty heading first to the port of *La Spezia*. There they would load up the wagon, two horses and the two men on the large schooner that Masso leased, to take them directly to *Messina* and the La Barbra's own warehouse docks. The four- daytrip gave them a chance to really get to know one another and it was on the first day the subject of the wagon and its spoils came up.

"Well Masso, it is just you and me and this big dark sea so tell me now. Where did you get this wagon and its contents? It is quite a haul, and it must come from very wealthy properties and churches. Your guys were in battles, I know that for sure and not in areas that would produce this kind of wealth, so what's the story?"

"An old wise man once said, 'for every action, a reaction is to follow', that's what happened. Do you remember my telling you how I had been wounded?"- And with that statement, Masso began telling the story. Except in the end he failed to mention the silver bullion under the seat.

The man just stood there, taking in the story, thinking, this boy is the luckiest person I have ever known and he is no accident. "So who was the wise old man?"

"The same one who said all the time, "He who controls the lemon controls the world', do you know who it was?" asked Masso?

"If I had said I not heard that statement less than ten thousand times in my life. I am lying, so it can only be Don Leonardo La Barba's statement. My father believed in his brother and until he turned everything over to Francis and the twins. Thing were great and getting better each year. You need to know Francis had you assigned to my division. He wanted me to make sure you would run away and desert. If that did not work, I was to make sure you died in or out of combat. Of course what Francis did not count on, was you. Masso, you did not just walk into the army, but thrived. You've somehow made it work for you. When you nutted the old cook you won the respect of the whole unit. But it was your organization and training skills of your Spartan warriors and what your group accomplished that was beyond words. You five guys changed the balance of the war through your strategies. You are Alexander the Great reborn or something like that's for sure."

"Why do you think the Don stepped down and turned everything over to Francis when he was only twenty one, and with so little experience?" Masso asked.

"I once asked my father once the same question. He just looked at me with such painful eyes, shook his head and shrugged his shoulders. Then said, "Some things come with big prices," and he just walked away. Maybe you can get him to tell you the whole story. All he has told my brothers is, "that's the way it is, so we put up or find something else to do". I found something else to do," Arturo answered smugly.

The two men repacked the wagon, and made note of each item, guessing where it might come from, its potential value. "I know this candelabra and it comes from the Basilica of San Nicolo outside Lecco by Lake Como," Arturo spoke up. We could contact the church about our find then try for a reward or ransom?"

"Or option number two, return this item for gratis and hope it can buy us some political favors that we can collect in the future with the mother church." Masso offers as an alternative choice.

Masso also spent time with the boats crew and captain finding the principals of sailing as a boy very interesting. The concept of the wind blowing against the sails was simple but to use the wind as the bird's wings do, lifting and pulling at the same time. The sails being the wings of the ship, lifting her across the water as she crisscrossed across the wide open liquid spaces. The nights had the best stars by the millions covering the sky above, the same ones he viewed all his life, but these nights they were brighter and clearer than he could ever remember before.

The arrival in Messina to the La Barba, Luccus docks was as uneventful as one would expect for an early Sunday morning. "I'll stay here and help unload the horses while you surprise your family." Masso waved his newest crew member off.

Over an early Sunday meal, a confused La Barba clan sat around the large family dining room table everyone in their place except with Masso at the head of the table, where Don Arturo normally sat or the Don when he was visiting.

"We welcome you into our humble home Abortrador De la Rosa. My son Arturo has given us some information about you and your appointment. It really does not surprise me knowing how cleaver my brother Leonardo is..was any way. You'll have to forgive us for staring but we remember you as the young boy in the background. The one Leo spent so much of his precious time with." The welcoming Don Arturo gave his guest a welcome that was not overly warm and a bit skeptical but understandable to Masso.

"Don Arturo, thank- you for opening your home to me. I never expected to have the honor to sit at my Patron's extended family's table…let alone share a meal with them. I must thank you again Madam La Barba, for the invitation."

For the next hour food was passed, wine drunk and the conversation as light as it could when discussing the work we did. "Sir, most of the time, it was just monotonous. The combat parts were few and really just came in the end." Masso kept to real basics and described it in the most general of terms. After dinner the five men went to the company's office.

"So tell us Abortrador De la Rosa, what are your plans to rescue our dying business?" the Don's brother had many of the old Don's mannerisms and his ability to cut to the bone when discussing business.

"I understand you worries, first about the business, second about me. I have already started to put in short term plans and long terms one. The exact actions I'm not ready to discuss, but know my one jobs is to clean up the messes and put things back to right, and to set the family back on strong footing, and with my plans we can do so. We are going to have to work together and to do that sir; you're going to have to trust me. At least trust the Don in knowing what he was doing in giving me this job, agreed?" The Don s younger brother head slowly nodding and so Masso took the time to ask the question everyone in the room wanted to know the answer to. "Don Arturo only you know why your brother turned over the business totally it seems to Francis. It just does not have any reason?"

"I guess you need to know the total story so you can deal with the truth. Our family has been on this land since the very early seventeen hundreds. My great grandfather Roberto La Babra was some low ranking Count and the estate had been a gift from the King as a bonus for some kindness he had received from his cousin. His son, my grandfather Georgeo took the estate and grew it to three times what it is now. He planted the trees and could pull fruit from his orchard like no one I have ever known, and his philosophy was, 'you cannot have too much land- it is the only asset worth holding'. He also started the La Barbra trading company. Unfortunately our father Arturo senior was a drunk, a gambler and a womanizer. When he was alive Leo and I worked all day to make the estate run like the old man Georgeo had done before us, but in ten years' time Arturo senior had lost most all of the estate and its income sources. So he traded Leonardo to the Luccus family, in away. Leo was to marry Paola Luccus when he turned twenty, who was the twin's older spinster sister. The Luccus's then would pay off Don Arturo senior debits and save the portion of the estate that is left. Lastly they agreed to put additional money back into the struggling trading company. The only other caveat was, when Leo and Paola had their first male child, and when that child, Francis, became of age, he and Paola's twin brothers Mario and Santo would take over all the businesses. Before the contract could be signed, our father died. So the family's Abortrador at the time, Augusta, took over and in the end, put one extra stipulation. All the moneys and accounting was to go through me and my side of the family. He made sure we had a place at the table too. So you see Don Leonardo did what he had to, and he married that woman. We both worked the next twenty years constantly putting back and diversifying the families holding. Then one day, he was forced out by the contract when Frances was twenty one. He spent years trying to come up with a plan to defeat that contract. You must have been his last play, and what he was able to come up with, so it looks like he has put all of our lives in your hands, so I sure hope you plan's works." The story finally told by Don Arturo.

"Well that explains a lot, and helps me understand a few finer points of this job and why he gave it to me. With your permission I would like to review the books, and a list of assets, including the ones Francis and company have sold since he took control of the Don's personal business. I know he leased the estate to a Palermo family for 20 years including the harvest. I want to see if maybe, because he had no legal rights to sell or lease without the Don being dead, I can salvage any of it back. I also think the docks need full time management to cut down on loses. It can be a service we offer all the warehouses and trading companies. It will pay for itself. For a flat monthly fee we make sure thief is not happening. We are going to start slow and we will ruff up some old idea's but trust me La Barba trading company or if need be a new... La Barba and Son's trading company will be a power to be dealt with soon, yes very soon. So now where are those books?"

The night was filled lots of page turning and questions asked, that they were not expecting. "When does the lease for the mine expire? How much is our Sulphur bringing in the current market and what is the labor cost? How much did the shipping business in *Agrigento* bring in the last five years? Are they turning business away or just getting by?" Masso's questions showed Don Arturo, that his son's choice to trust this boy was correct. Masso was his brother's spirt alive for sure. Though a big gamble for them all and there still was one thing that seriously concerned him. Something he did not think his brother considered, something he would have to make his own plan for?

The next morning Father Stefano appeared as he was asked to by Masso to join him and Don Arturo at his family's bank's front door that morning. "Stefano what brings you here? Don Arturo, good morning please come in." *What's going on here*? The banker asked himself as he opened the bank's front door. *Why are they here without notice? Why is Stefano here with them and why is Don Leonardo's ferocious looking bastardo with them?* All were questions the banker was asking himself before turning around nervously, "Please into my office, I'll be just be a few moments to get the coffee and…"

"Excuse me sir, but my name is Tomasso Del la Rosa," Masso extended his hand and for a moment Felix froze. All eyes were on the extended hand. When the pause became embarrassing the banker took it with a brief shake already dreading what he feared would come. *Oh where was that weasel brother of mine when you need him? He needs to deal with whatever shit storm they are about to hit us with.* "Well please sit, I'll be right back," but Masso stood in his way.

 "If Mr. Goldin you would let me finish my statement, we all can get down to business, then coffee. The La Barba family has been doing business with your family's bank for a long time. It also owes your bank a lot of money. So depending on your future answers and attitude, will determine on whether the family continues to do business with you in the future or ever pays you one lira more."

"Let me explain Felix, the day before Don Leonardo was attacked. He summoned Masso and I to his office. In the short of it, he appointed Masso, tobe the La Barba's family's Abortrador." Father Stefano already knew this news was going to be a difficult situation for his brother Felix. Who was not good at handling problems and this was going to be a big problem.

Felix quickly looked at his own brother in total disbelief, "Is this true brother? You actually there, saw it with your own eyes? Why would the Don do that, a Bastardo?"

"It would be wise my younger brother to show the La Barba family's new head some respect. As of now, anything Masso asks or tells you consider it as if it was the Don himself here saying it, do you understand?"

"What can the Goldin Bank do for you Mr. Del la Rosa, sir, it will be our greatest pleasure."

"Let's start by looking at every transaction the bank has been involved in with any of the Don's personal accounts, and all the transactions of Luccus and La Barba trading. I want to see whatever notes you're holding and any receivables you have against those notes. I want the last five years of Francis accounts as well. Let's start there and work backwards. One more thing Mr. Goldin, the Don had set me up a personal account to help fund a special project he has me working on, would you please get me that cash?"

The padre left the two men with his brother, knowing several people were not going to be very happy when this day ended.

Feeling on top of the world after his afternoon's shave and haircut older brother Hector, was day- dreaming as he approached his bank. *A quick walk through the bank then an early dinner with my mistress, she is so sweet, young and her passions well...* "What in the name of Jesus and the holy moth... What's going on here, Felix are you crazy? Get these men out of here."

"Mr. Golden come in and stop your foul tongue from wagging, or I'll come out of this chair and stop it myself. Now Felix explain to your brother, who and what I am. Then explain to you're older brother that he needs to smarten up."Masso's patience was beginning to thin out the more he dealt into the conspiracy.

The two brothers were off in a corner for just a few moments with the mention of Abortrador and Fathers Stefano's personal visit to confirm. The two men looked like death was facing them both. It was not just their future but the whole scattered Goldin family network. People who were funding and depending on returns for those moneys invested. "He wants the cash the Don had set up in that independent account. You know the one you turned over to Frances at first but which you have been putting into your own pocket the last three years?"

"Ok you two from what we have seen from these books and documents you and your bank are up to your ass in some serious problems. You used assets of Don Leonardo's personal estate to cover Francies loans, and…."

"No that's not right, they were covering the trading company's loans, and." Hector interrupted.

"Wrong, again. What did I tell you about taking? These notes are not to La Barba trading or to Luccus La Barba trading. No these are made out to Francis La Barba, period. Any loan you have made using the Dons personal assets need to be called in. If those assets have been liquidated they need to be repurchased or cash paid in full for the sale of that asset. If it was given away under the fair market price you will make it right. You owe me personally, how much was it Felix? Yes plus interest. The money you have made off these deals will be given back as well. You will as of this moment no longer do any business except to collect what you can on your notes with them. You tell Francis nothing about me, I'll confront him soon enough, do you both understand?"

"Mr. Del la Rosa, we don't have the cash to do as you request, and we have our own investors to report to. What are you going to do take us to court? It will be years and…" *"Smack"*, was the sound of Masso's open hand slapping Hector's face and whipping his head sideways.

"I told you to keep your mouth shut, if you don't agree fine. I then will be dealing with your younger brother here, because you will no longer be walking among us. If your brother doesn't agree, well the whole banking world, and, as far as I can reach out will know how your entire family are Murano Jews not Catholics. Your investors will not like that, so the choice is yours."

The last hour was spent working out the details of how Don La Barba's estate would take only forty percent of the bank stock in return for all money owed the Don. Masso got for his money due him, the near worthless notes of Francis, moneys he personally still owed the bank, a total of over twenty thousand lira.

At the same time Arturo is heading back to *Palermo* to take over the Dons care and begin his future life as the new face of the La Barba family. He also knew it was only going to be a short time before he would be confronted by Francis and company. With the family Abortrador's written orders in his possession Arturo also knew he would have the upper hand. He just hoped he could delay the face to face long enough for Masso's plans to have time to take root. He knew his cousin was not going to like any part of it, especially. Art's chuckle grew to a full belly laugh as he thought of this part of Masso's brilliant plan, "Poor Frances," he said out loud.

From *Messina* Masso took the wagon south to the large seaport town of *Catania*. The ship captain had told him of this jewel of a port in a conversation one evening, "Of all the port cities I have traveled to in my twenty three years on these waters, *Catania* is my favorite. A quiet and welcoming port, full of beauty, lots of products from all over the world. The city has some very old families who are still doing business successfully and yet there is room for new comers too."

When Masso had a chance he asked, "Who is the third wealthiest family on that list?"

The captain with a very puzzled look asked, "Why just that one?"

"The first family has it locked down just with the fact they have been doing it the longest. The second family has already lost ambition, satisfied where they are or they would be number one. But the third family I bet is still ambitious wanting more, to be first. Those are the people I want on my side." Masso answered, making note of the captain's answer.

"You are right. The Alceu family is the most aggressive of the three. Carmine is the head of the family. He grew up hustling on the docks, and he put the Alceu family back in power. His son Gabriel is much more conservative."

So with a plan slowly fermenting in his mind Masso headed to that eastern jewel port, which may become the family's new home, *Catania*.

Like most people with some age to them Carmine Alceu found comfort in routine, which included a quite late lunch at *Bartellis'* most weekdays. So in his best clothes Masso followed him in and without invitation sat down moments after the old man had sat down. "Good afternoon Don Alceu. I hope you don't mind my intrusion and will allow me to purchase your lunch, today. I understand they have the best eggplant casserole, which is what I am having and what looks interesting to you this afternoon?"

The old man looked at this very young man with the scared face and determined presence, and in a quick choice answered. "My interest was to eat alone, but maybe I don't know all my options, which are Mister?"

"Well sir, you could call the owner and ask him to throw me out. Then you then could enjoy a fine meal on me and go back to work full. Or you can still enjoy a fine meal, share a tale or two and listen to an idea to move your families company from third place to second maybe even first. My name is Tomasso Del la Rosa recently retired from the Sardinian army after our victorious victories over the evil Austrians. My organization The Alliance is looking to start a bank to fund our growing businesses."

"Mr. Del la Rosa, why do you need me to help you start a bank? I can tell by your forwardness that you have a plan but my guess, no money and you think by purchasing my lunch. I will listen to a wonderful cannot- miss idea, I will fund your project, am I right?"

"No sir, we actually had some funds to start our going enterprises. We believe citrus, especially lemons will be a very profitable business. The Alliance is bringing together small and medium farmers into our group and then we sell as a co-op, bigger is better. The time will come when even our funds can't cover all the money needs. We want to be able to offer these orchards loans, to cover expansions and revitalization. Of course these loans will be secured by their property as collateral. We will also be providing property protection to all in our alliance members and to any one in need, for a price. The need is great, what with bandits and all being such a threat these days. So addition men are needed, and we have to train them, and that requires payroll and then warehouse space on a dock, see where this is going? Now what we do bring to the offer is three thousand pounds of Spanish silver bullion, and twenty thousand dollars of notes at 4.575% from Frances La Barba. We have just opened a political branch in *Palermo* and now want to move into beautiful *Catania*. Who better to join forces with than the hungriest people in town, am I right?"

The old Don said nothing at first but waved the owner over, "Bartelli my friend, I want to introduce you to *Catania's* newest businessmen. He has just returned from the war and was just about to tell me the story of his scares. Please bring us two of my specials, if you'll allow me to order for us Mr. Del la Rosa."

"My friends call me Masso and this is your *restaurante*."

Over lunch they talked about the war and Masso gave a short version and how it was he who had planned and implemented the actions that won the real war in the end. The deal was a brutal battle over two days, though the bolts of silk Masso sent the Don's wife that night really closed the deal. A new bank was chartered by the Alceu family with 15% ownership and with a commitment of over million pounds with most loans needing heavy collateral before lending. The alliances employees also were to protect the banker's own family's properties. The silver and most of the war spoils were left as the committed investment of the new Alceu and Alliance Commercial Bank.

The last part of the trip home passed not too far for the family's sulphur lease, so Masso made it his next planned destination. The sun was way past lunch when he stopped early for the day. After tending the horse, he set up a quick camp then went out hunting with his sling. Off to his right down in the small valley was where the gash in the hillside was the mouth of the sulfur mine. The area to the left led toward several small groves of trees with fields of high grasses in-between them, and the ground had slight swells of different heights.

Now this looks like a good place to find dinner, Masso thought to himself. He pulled his trusty leather weapon out and he crouched down at a tree line edge to pick up a couple stones and to watch for any movements or signs. *With time all things will come to you,* Masso thought to- him-self. Out to his left hopped a big buck rabbit, stone, sling, winding in harmony like so many times before, and just before he launched his stone, an arrow whizzed by, just missing the rabbit. Knowing by instinct the animal only had two choices as to which way to jump, Masso chose left, which was also the now dead rabbit's choice too.

Out of the tree line above him came a boy with a bow in his hand, running as hard as his legs would carry him, running right past Masso and not even seeing him. The boy then threw his bow across the rabbit trying to hold it from getting away.

"You know that is my kill boy?" Masso came out, the sling still in his hand.

"Oh, I thought maybe I stunted it, I did not even see you there, sir. We, my family really need this kill. I'll help you find another but,

but," and the boy began crying. "We haven't eaten any meat in a week and my…."

"All right, stop crying. Let's see what more we can find with the two of us looking." Even when the two spent the next couple of hours hunting the best they could end up with, was only a couple doves and a mud hen but Masso did find some wild turnips and mushrooms to add for the harvest." Ok Paolo you take the rabbit and mud hen, leave me the two doves, take some of the turnip with the green tops and I'll just take one of these mushrooms. You take the rest. I expect you to meet me back here at sunrise and take me through the mine and then we are even." They even shook on it, and the boy ran off happily into the night.

As promised just as the sun broke the horizon Paolo appeared. "Good morning Masso, my mother sent you a bit of fresh bread for your morning meal and she gives her most humble thanks. You saved my life in more than one way yesterday, and I thank you too."

"Sit and tell me what you know of the mine. There seems more activity at night than during the day. Why is that?"

"The mine is almost played out. The numbers of workers are maybe fifteen total for both crews, that are if one of the young boys has not died, then less until he is replaced. I guess the price for sulfur is much greater than human life. The few areas in the mine that they are still mining are deep below ground, in shallow crevasses. It's a lot of hammering for a chunk here or there. Why are you interested in that old hole Masso?"

"Because, my young friend I am in the hunt for an old hole, and maybe this one would do?" As they walked down the road toward the opening Masso continued the questioning. "How long does it take to fill a rail car, and do you know where it is sent to?" Masso asked casually.

"Well the mine has not shipped anything out on the rails for years. It's by wagon- loads that the sulfur is being shipped out now. It is only down the road a mile or so to the Fenshaw operation, to the west of here. They have a full processing plant. Well here she is. It may take a moment for your eyes to adjust to the light and you will get use to the smell at least if you stay in here for very long. So what do you think? Is it what you're looking for?"

Masso's first impressions were not what he had hoped for, but the entrance was large, and the ceilings at least were twenty feet tall, and the cavern went deep into the hillside. They came to the large gaping hole in the floor, opening up to the bowels of hell. A wood ladders lead down to the next level, and then more ladders led down and down and down. The young boys who worked these holes climbed up and back down all day every day twelve hour shifts for a few liras a day. Money these poor kids labored for, was so, their own families could survive another day. *I was lucky that the army paid more for my body than these mines did or this would have been my fate too.*" Masso thought to himself. "Is it always this warm in here or does it ever cool off any time of the year?"

"Yes it is pretty much like this year round. Why does it matter? Besides what could you do here, but mine sulphur?"

"Empty spaces can be used to store things from the rain, wind, sun. The train tracks could make shipping those stored items, as needed, now can you see what I mean? I just need to find the owner and see." Masso left the thought hanging. "I guess this big hole to the lower levels could be boarded up and…"

"You're going to store what, and will you need help? I am a good worker and I bet my uncle would work you a good deal. It has to be better than his current holder, and then I would not have to work down there." Paolo lite up when he heard of an alternative to what he thought to be his fate.

"Your uncle," Masso turned to the boy, "your family owns the property here and you're scrapping for food? Your uncle, where is he, somewhere around here?"

"Sure he lives with us. My mom takes care of him. He is getting old and frail, but he is pretty much still all there if you know what I mean. Follow me if you're serious."

 The short walk back to Paola's home, gave Masso a chance to prepare a campaign. "Don Cheezo , my Name is,"

"Yes I remember you, from Del la Rosa, right? The last time you were here I gave you much too easy terms. If you want to work our land it will cost you ten percent more or I'll lease it to any one of the many men who wants it, do you understand? Ten percent not any less, take it or leave it."

Masso turned toward Paola and his mother and smiled, "He thinks I am someone else, someone from his past, but he is right about the current based on production." Masso writes down his offer and passes it to the old man. "I am prepared to pay you Don Cheezo, this much each month, just for the land lease. This is no matter what production is. Plus I will give you a ten percent increase for each load of sulfur shipped out of the mine." Masso then looked back to the boy and his mom who had tears in her eyes.

The Luccus La Barba books showed Masso, when he reviewed them. That an average of two and a half wagon loads were coming out of the mine per day six days a week. What Masso found in reality was actually six total loads go out a day. A couple loads during the day, but also three or four at night. These nighttime loads were not being reported on anyones books, so Masso concluded someone was stealing almost one hundred loads a month from the Chezzo's but also from the La Barba family. A visit to Fenshaw would lead back to, the sulphur mine's manager.

 "My name is Masso Del La Rosa and I am here on the behest of Don Leonard La Barba to get back the payments you owe him for the one- hundred and fifty wagon loads a month you have sold under your name. For how many years has this been going on, five or is it seven?"

"I don't know who you think you're fooling, boy. The Don is not talking to anybody, and if he was talking, he would not have sent you." Masso was now close to the man. His right fist hit deep into the fat man's stomach, knocking most of the air out of his weakened body. This also dropped the man to his knees. Masso's left hand then easily grabbed and pulled the hair of the now gasping for breath man's head backwards. In his right hand, Masso had a bright shiny revolver, whose barrel was easily inserted forcefully inside the terrified man's mouth.

 "Do you want to bet you thieving piece of donkey dung, that I will not pull this trigger of my *pistola* that's in your mouth. That is exactly what is going to happen if you don't give me the truthful answers to the questions I am about to ask? Do you understand? A simple nod up and down will do." The man briefly nodded.

Masso slowly pulled the revolver out of the broken man's mouth and slapped him backwards.

"Please don't kill me. I did not want anything to do with this. I told Francis that when he came to me about six months before the Don's attack. He said he was running everything with the Don you know not in the business anymore. He offered me two choices take the deal or find myself another job. Look I have been here eight years. I was only getting five percent of the gravy. The rest, I sent directly to Francis."

"Well from now on send it all to the Don's new bank." Masso handed him a business card with the new banking instruction. "One more thing your pay is cut fifteen percent." Masso then pulled the man up by his collar and sent him running.

The rest of the trip home from the mine, Masso took the opportunity to finish formulating the next step of the plan for the property. *I will not need that weak manager for much longer. This storage location is perfect. Incoming produce can be stored until we have enough to ship two or three rail cars full at a time, to Catania. It will save us money and time.*

As Masso rode through the ancient town's central plaza with its bright-blue and yellow tile fountain he noticed it had not changed much. What he did notice, was many of the old store fronts had a refreshed look. A new coffee bar was now open where the bakery had been. The new bigger bakery was a block over, just down the street from the Black Rose Inn.

A man was sitting, out front of the Black Rose, in a chair smoking a pipe. He looked vaguely familiar, but not someone Masso recognized. He nodded at the man as he walked into the inn. "Where is the proprietor of this bug infested dump? I have a complaint!" He shouted as he walked through the entrance. No one greeted him, no one was in sight.

"I am the manager here sir." A voice came from behind Masso. "What seems to be the problem Mr. Del la Rosa? Is your room not acceptable? Maybe you would rather have one with a better view I would be happy to accommodate you."

Masso turned toward the voice which rang a bell from the past, though he noted the man walked past him with a serious limp of his left leg. Then he noticed that when the inn keeper reached for a key, he favored his left hand. The right arm did not seem to work very well. But it was only after the proprietor turned to face Masso with his key, that Masso finally recognized this man and realized who he was and when they last met. Back then he was with a partner. It was so many life times' ago. His attention was now on alert.

"I know you don't I, from Four Corners, what ten years ago or so? You and your fat friend, right?"

"Yes sir, the worst day, and maybe the luckiest day of my life. I'm really sorry for taking the job all those years ago. We were told to just scare you. To take the bag and not to hurt you, just kind of rough you up if necessary, but not really hurt you. He did not tell us you were a trained warrior. We were being a test, of sorts. When you stuck the staff into Jeffry's face I got scared I just rushed you with the knife to scare you off. The next thing I knew I couldn't walk, and my right elbow was killing me."

A visual memory came flashing back. It was as clear to Masso as if it happened only yesterday.

 "Did you know the Don paid for Jeffry's funeral and some cash to his mom? Me he gave me a promise ofa job for life. I know you have no reason to trust me but if the things that occurred that day-…. Well if they had not happened then my life would have led me to more bad choices, which, in my case would have certainly led me to an early grave by now. In the end you saved my life sir. Anyway the Don promised me this job, and you are now his voice in this. Rizzo told me that the decision would be up to you. I will give you all I have, I promise you that sir. My name is Roberto Rosso by the way. Anything you need just say the word."

"So Roberto what's for dinner and where is the crew?"

"I'll check with Mrs. O'Malley. She's a bit off, but a great cook. And if you have something special you want, or say, liked prepared a certain way, she will be happy to try to make it for you. Do you want me to get her to make you something now?"

"No Roberto, I am fine, but if you would ask her to fix something special for Thursday night, we are going to have a small celebration for about eight."

 "Of course, of course, Rizzo and Charlie are over at the casino over seeing some workers. It's down the old Mustard Road heading out of town, towards Four Corners."

 Masso first made a stop down the street, to the town's bakery. "Good morning Miss Leasa, and how is my favorite baker this day?"

"Masso, come in, I heard you were coming back. You look so grown up. You're no longer the mischievous little boy, but a handsome young man? How is Mella I have not seen her in a while?"

Miss Leasa, besides being the towns' oldest baker, was also the town's busiest body. If there was something worth knowing she knew it. "Mella is Mella never ages, always busy, but I will tell that you asked about her. I am on my way out to see her shortly. I thought though I might stop by and find what's really going on around here. That is, if you are still the lady in the know? "

"You know I am and what do you want to know?"

"Everything," The next half hour, Miss Leasa and Masso talked of the past before she began filling him in on what has happened up until the present.

"Masso, that man who lives in your family's estate, he is an evil man. He acts like he is some sort of royalty, demanding privileges, including sexual ones from brides, before he will grants them permission to marry. You need to do something, this is your hometown, and."

"Yes ma'am, I heard that before, and I am working on it. In the meantime Miss Leasa, if you get something juicy or important let me know first."

 Masso easily found the stand alone building. There were lots of men coming and going out of both front and back doors.

"I like what you got done here in such a short time, how long till we open Rizzo?" Masso asked as the two men hugged one another.

"It's really good to see you too boss. As far as this place, we should be ready to open the bar and big casino by next weekend. The wheel game is due the first of next week. We already have had a few regulars without even opening the doors yet. If you still want a stage, we left room back in that corner, see? Rizzo turned and pointed to the empty space. "We also have room behind the building to add a kitchen if you think we need one. I think it should be more of a man's place than a whorehouse. But with that said, there are six rooms upstairs if you want to bring women in."

Masso walked around. "This is not what I had in my head, but it works well. The bar along one wall instead in the middle works better. It gives more counter space for drinkers. Yeah and like you said, I don't think we need to add working women yet, even if we have space. Has Charlie been any help, or did he disappear as soon as I left?"

"No, actually Masso he is the one who worked the lay out plan and ordered the wheel game and the gambling supplies. I guess he did pick up some knowledge for his lost wages." Rizzo replied in his keenly observant way.

"So my friend what shall we call her, The Men's Club?" Masso asked?

"Actually, we have been calling her *Molti Soldi* from the start among ourselves any way." A reply behind him came. Smiling with a grin ear to ear was Gerome, as he joined the other two.

Big Money, I like it. Well you guys have done a great job in just a short matter of time, but how did we end up with the two buildings instead of one?" Masso turned back to look at Rizzo, his concern was mostly about cash out lay not planned for.

"You met, or should I say reacquainted yourself with Roberto at the Inn? When we first came to town he was the man Father Stefano suggested we talk to first. It turns out Don Leonardo owns the Black Rose Inn. He had bought it to keep his promise to Roberto about a job. So the Black Rose cost us nothing and a nicer environment to call home then here, don't you think? Mrs. O'Malley is a great cook. You're going to love her cooking. She reminds me of my sweet dead mother's meals and none of us has to cook or even cut potatoes. Back to point anyway, we got this old building. It cost more than we had planned for, but there were not a lot of buildings available which fit our needs. I gave him a little hard silver down and a promissory note for the rest. The papers are up in the office. I used the remaining cash to get supplies. We are almost done and almost broke." Rizzo explained. "Gerome and Divain have been out every day and have several orchards who were very interested in more information."

"Yeah when I mention the potential of arranging loans to improve or expand their orchards, they were like a teenage girl in- love,… easy." Divain brags as he walked in the back door. "Welcome to *'Molti Soldi'*, boss. "

"Well my friends you have out done my expectations. My time too has produced results. I will go over it with you all at the meeting Thursday, Rizzo get a message to Don Arturo La Barba and request his presence as well. Divain did you find Mella and Augusto?" Masso asked.

"She is living in a little hut up by the Allaya's lake like you thought. I called on her right after we got here and told her you were well and will see her as soon as you get back. I'm sorry to say, Augusto died shortly after you left. Mella seemed all right. She is still collecting all those plants."

Though the trip out to the lake was not back to his home, it did have a familiar feel to it, from the moment he walked into the hut. The sights of hanging plants everywhere and the thousand different smells brought him back to a comfortable and simpler time. "The man said you would be by, and that you are well. Come over to the light and let me see you boy. Oh my son, what have they done to your face?" The next several hours were spent getting caught up on what had happened in both of their lives. Mella went on and on about local gossip about this person or that much Masso had already gotten from Miss Leasa. She finally got around to discussing a seriously big problem with the new Don of Del la Rosa. "This diablo who lives in our manor is a sick man. He is a sexual predator, demanding the virginity of every girl before granting them permission to wed, like he was a king or something. I heard he raped a twelve- year- old. She was the daughter of the Bishop of Palermo. His family the Narisis', were forced to send him away. We were the misfortune, to that decision. The family unleashes him on us. I tell you there is not one women or girl safe with him out loose free to do his evil. Now that you're here, what are you going to do about it?"

"Has he come looking for love from you too?" Masso teased.

 "Is that any way to talk to your old mother young man? You know you're not so old that Mella couldn't pull your pants down and smack your bottom."

"Yes Mama, your right. It's not something to jest about. Did this man have anything to do with Augusto's death?"

"When the new Don came in, he fired most everyone and just let the estate including the trees go to waste. He did not harvest what did grow and beat anyone who took any. Augusto had nothing to do. The new Don did not want to meet about estate needs or issues with the property. So the old man just climbed in bed one day, and never left it. He died in less than a month. It was so sad to watch his light go out a little more every day. He was just a shell of himself I'm glad you were not here to see it. So what are your plans my boy?"

"I heard the same information from Miss Leasa earlier today. She sends her regards by the way. I do have a plan to put things back together and will be happy to discuss it with you over dinner. That is if that' what I think is in that pot on the fire?"

 As they ate Masso slowly laid out his plans, he explained what he had done and what he still needed to do, Mella reviewed each step of the plan, asking a few questions, and making a few suggestions, "I think it is a well thought out strategy and it gives you room to adjust. I like it my boy and the Don I am sure would approve if he could. You have become a wise little fox my son. Don Leonardo was clever to put the family's future in your hands. It is just like when the Don's grandfather put the La Barba family future in Augusto's hands. Now come outside so I can treat your scars which are a mess." Which Mella did lovingly.

It had been pouring down rain all night before the meeting, but with morning light a new clean fresh day faced them all. Don Arturo arrived early to make a deal with Masso. They would have his support, but only if the Don could get a commitment for just one stipulation from Masso , that he needed first.

Masso began the meeting with the good news. "I have secured financing for the Alliance with the Alceu family of *Catania*. We are actively looking for a dock and warehouse space now. I want you, Don Arturo, to abandon the two offices and just leave everything there. Move to *Catania* and open La Barba and Son's Trading. The only way for the family to survive is to cut out the infection before it kills everything. Let Francis have everything but without you all he has is three offices, two docks and two near empty warehouses. He also has creditors and no friendly lenders.

"We as a family and me especially, as the lone working survivor of the original family, have given your offer a lot of thought. Here is what I suggest we do. Close the *Massina* office and stop all of Luccus and LaBarba shipping out of there. We still need the *Scilla* location, if nothing it shows, your office as Abortrador is in good faith. Also in the same good faith, I need you to marry an older woman." He looked Masso straight into his face while speaking. "We trust your desire to do what's best for the family today. With that said, it is for the years in the future that we also need assurances. That no matter what you do, you will not take over everything to promote your own family. To do that, you must marry someone who cannot produce you any legal heirs. Maybe she could be someone who also can help you in your social standing. It is a pivotal issue for us. If that is agreeable for you then Alberto will man the new offices, Antonio stays in the main land office AJ is in *Palermo* so we will have La Barba presence in all three locations, that is, if you agree."

The request totally took Masso by surprise. At seventeen the thought of marriage was the furthest thing on his mind. 'Think fast, think, think, think. "Do you have someone in mind, or do I have a say?"

"Actually my wife's sister, Lady Serafina Mayo, she is a widow with no children. Her people come from an ancient Sicilian family, well respected. She can help you dress better and learn a few social graces. Most importantly she will introduce you to the right people, people you'll need to know."

"I don't need those things and if people don't like me because of a birth issue I had no control over that. So then, up their asses with their options. Now Don Arturo, I do understand your concern, so let's say, when I get old enough to get married, and if I should marry. Mrs. Mayo will be my choice. That is the best I can do." So a deal was stuck, sight unseen and another piece of the plan was put in place. Like the Don's, another winless deal for the betterment of the family.

Over the best shared dinner the original six had ever had together, the mood was buoyant and full of bluster. The second half of the evening was much more serious. "Tonight we are gathered here as the charter members of our new society. I ask each of you to make a blood oath to **Our Thing** the **Alliance**. In doing so you are making a personal commitment to put no other business over that of our **Alliance,** not even your own families." Masso being the first to say the oath, "I Masso Del La Rosa do at this time give my total support, financially, physically and without second thought to Our Thing the Alliance and all of her business. May this blood I shed today be proof of this commitment." The small dagger cut his trigger finger. Each of the men one at a time followed suit saying the words, and letting of blood sealed their pledge.

As the group were finishing the last few days' worth of touches on the '*Melti Soldi* or Big Money', Masso takes his first trip out to solicitous members of the Citrus Alliance. His first stop was to visit Don Tito Delfino, his Patron's friend and co-conspirator to the original idea.

As Masso approached the estate this time the view seemed more unkempt. Trees were loaded with fruit, but the grounds did not look pristine like his first visit.

Lucia greeted him as he rode up, "Well it has been a while Masso. Last we heard you were in the army fighting Austrians. Considering all and all, you know, you still don't look too bad. You still have all your hands and feet and except for the scars on your face. You look more like a grown man. Much better than the last time you were here. Now what brings the war hero here?"

"I came to see your dad to talk with him about his and Don Leonardo's plan for the Citrus Union, and...."

"My father passed away sixteen months ago Masso. He just did not show up for his early breakfast one morning and he was found dead in the bed. He must have died in his sleep. It has been a difficult year for sure. Of course Enrico is as useless as tits on a boar. When he's not out raising hell with his worthless friends he still does very little work. Did you notice the way the orchards look? My father is screaming from his grave. He would have never neglected them as Enrico has. All he does is when he is here, is walk around giving orders like he is the grand Duke of Delfino. He got the title sof Don now, but if I were not over seeing everything we would have gone broke ten times already. He came into the office yesterday saying he has already sold our crops and the contract crops to the Florino family. Those lucky pig farmers have him so wrapped around their finger, they tell him anything and he just agrees an then he comes back and tells him. Don Carmine Florino says this is the only right way to do this or that. Then Agosto says, they have the biggest orchard in the area. So they get the best prices for their fruit and because he is his closest friend they will give him the special price? How can they give him any price when the market has not even opened yet? The price he accepted is so low we will probably lose money on this year's crops. He knows nothing because he only wants the title but not the work it takes to make a farm to run. I really don't know what to do."

Masso takes a few moments before he speaks. "Lucia, I am so sorry for your loss of you father, I was really looking forward to working with him, to pick up on his knowledge, but that is not going to happen now. So the crop here on the property is your brother's - that is the law. The contracts your father has set up with the smaller growers are not Enrico's to do with, and you physically hold them, right? So what I suggest is that you give your brother until February 15th to complete the picking. It will be his job to hire and oversee the harvest or you will do it. It's has to be that date so the fruit does not over- ripen and become near worthless. The Florino family will not risk trying to bully a member of our Alliance. So next year you will not have this problem. Then if they do try, well it will be their last time, enough said. I'll come back right after the harvest and we can hold a meeting of your group. They will come in under your umbrella. You will still control your people but as a head of this Alliance family. You pay a percentage for us to handle security, and the sale of your harvests. Our prices I promise you will be the best the markets will bear.”

“You’re right and I bet he can’t get enough pickers at this late date to do the work in the time left. Clever, and yet he is going to go crazy, but nothing more than threats and screaming. He can’t do anything but that. Thank you for the good advice.”

On the way back home Masso decided to stop back by the mine site, to do a few measurements to see just how much real useable space he will have to work with and how much area in the back was going to need to be covered. He stopped first to check up with the Cheezo family to make sure they were getting weekly moneys from mine.

“Masso what brings you this way today? Are you ready to put your plan into action? Do you need help?” The young Paolo boy was excited at the new possibilities.

“I’m just here to take a few measurements, but sure, come along and you can tell me what has been going on around here since the last time I was here.”

“Well the mine office has been sending money weekly, but less per week than the previous week and from what I see it looks like she is pretty well empty, so your hole is just about ready for you. I cannot see it producing much more.”

When the two entered the mine it seemed to be unusually quiet, “something is off,” said young Paolo. “It’s too quiet. No one is working up here and I can’t hear any picks striking rocks below, can you?”

“It is strange that?”…. Before another word was uttered, the ground began shaking and knocked both of them down to the ground. Masso quickly realized they needed to be out of this hole, and fast. He jumped up even as the whole area still was moving, "we need to run, and now." Masso grabbed the boy by his shirt and half lifting and half dragging began the sprint. The ground stopped shaking but the two continued out toward the front. Moments later the second tremor was even angrier, and then, just as they reached the front entrance, a huge explosion took place deep down with in the bowels of the mine causing a power full belch of sulfur gas followed by a rumble so deep within the core of the earth that it seemed to awaken the devil himself. They had three choices, right toward the rail car, or straight ahead toward the road leading in and out, or left and up toward higher ground. Masso's gut pushes them to the left. They climbed as fast as the shaking ground allowed them to. The two rounded a corner when they encountered an old mine employee hiding in the rocks. Before anything could be said the whole area began to shake once again but differently and the gases coming out of the mine were increasing in volume and heat. Then like a drunk throwing up, the raw heated liquid sulfur began pouring out of the mine in heaves. The next half an hour the entire mine filled back in with replacement liquid yellow gold. Every pound taken out over the years was replaced and now even the front area including the rail tracks were being covered up with cooling mineral.

"What just happened here Masso? I never ever though I would see what we just witnessed. Looks like you're going to need a new storage hole though. Say Robby what are you doing here?"

"I was just following orders I did not know that was going to happen. *Please*, forget you ever saw me," and the old man began to stand up."

"I do not think so Robby," Paolo reached out and grabbed the man, who was visibly shaking like the ground. "Now tell us. Have you met Don Masso Del La Rosa here? He is the new lease holder, so I am sure he will want the full truth as to why you are up here and everything you know about what just happened."

The older man glanced first to the boy, then directly at the young man with the scarred face and soul penetrating dark green eyes. He thought to himself, those eyes can see the truth. He then peed himself. "I'm so sorry, I'm sorry, I'm so sorry," was all he kept saying until Masso slapped his face once.

 Gently but firmly Masso spoke, "Tell us what you know, leave nothing out and be sure to tell me the truth, do you understand? Nod your head."

The old man seemed to come back from wherever he had been and slowly he began, "I have worked the mine for over twenty five years and for the last twelve I have been the demolition man. The mine has not needed me for over a year, but when Mr. Lawrence called on me, he said, he had a job for me. It was to blow up the mine when you sir were in the mine. I was to blow the whole mine up clapping itself inward. I had set the charge above the pit's hole, knowing the explosion should get the results he wanted. Mount Etna must have had a really massive earthquake today about the time you just entered the mine, knocking my charge down from the ceiling into the deeps of the hole and when it exploded it must have open something deep inside the earth, allowing the new liquid Sulphur, to come back to the surface."

They all three were now looking at a yard still filling with a golden yellow lake already half covering the lone left rail car it's tracks now buried deep within the Sulphur.

"Holy Mother of Christ," Paolo yelled out. "Well Masso, it looks like we are back in the mining business again, and in a very big way, what do you think?"

"*Yeah*, I guess I will just have to find somewhere else for that other need to be filled. This property will be mining for a long time to come and your family Paolo will not go hungry ever again. Let's climb around to move away from this heat and smell. You old man should be dead, but your actions right or wrong produced this, so today you live."

By the time they got back to his cart people from all around the area were out, and arrived by walking, riding in carriages, wagons or carts. They came to be healed. Some came looking for a religious experience but most came just wanting to share the miracle. In all of the excitement nobody noticed to absence of Mr. Lawrence the mine's previous manager.

 When confronted for the second time, he started talking like a possessed man the moment he saw Masso standing in front of him. "Please let me explain. When Francis did not get his money after two weeks he came to visit. He came to find out why? He blew up and started hitting me, yelling obscenities and threatening me. Then he really lost it when he heard that you now owned the mines lease. He really went crazy, claiming you stole it out from under him. Well if he could have, he would have killed me right then and there. Instead he forced me to hire someone to blow you up inside the mine the next time you came or he would make me pay for it."

"Well Mr. Lawrence," Masso said quietly, without emotion. "You could have respected me your employer by reaching out and letting me know. Then, I could have dealt with it, but you chose to fear him more than me, your last big mistake."

In years to come what had happen to Lawrence was a favorite guessing game for those who knew him. Was he in the mine when the miracle happened? Or, why did he leave just before the miracle? How unlucky was he? Then, what a bad choice he has made wonder if he even knows, was the most popular response?

This trip back home was one joyful time for Masso who now knew the Alliance had an unlimited amount of sulphur to mine. It was cash in the ground, just waiting to be plucked. "Yes I bet Francis went nuts when he learned I had the new lease. Now though, with the full mine to be re-harvested and, millions of lira lost to me. Maybe he will hang himself. Naw, it would be too easy and not much of chance of that happening any time soon."

 Paolo benefited from the event also, as he was quick to take advantage of the family's newest opportunity. They started a tourist business, which was now supplying the daily visitors whose numbers keeps growing, all who had come to view the miracle themselves. People came by any means possible. Many were sick, or dying. They were looking for a magical cure. Others came to pray at the site of what only could have been sent by God. Paolo would give his firsthand tale of the event. Space was used to build an inn and even open spaces were rented out for short term campers all for such a reasonable price.

At that s night's dinner back at the Black Rose the whole group sat down for one of Mrs. O'Malley's lamb stews, which was a big hit with everyone seated. "Gentlemen and I use that word loosely with this group," Charlie started his impromptu speech, "I would like to toast our fearless leader, who has made all this possible. It seems like only yesterday we were just potato peelers and," from the rest of the table moo's' and boo's erupted, "Alright, alright. To Masso, a better leader this group of misfits could not have asked for. To Masso, drink up."

"Thank you fellows and one more toast back, **to this Saturday night, Salute**." The rest of the night was filled with one toast after another until it got so ridiculous that they were toasting the King of Austria for starting the war, which brought them together in the first place.

Saturday morning was a buzz with finishing touches, Gerome was helping unloading the glassware, and overseeing their cleaning and the completion of the stage, where live entertainment that had been booked would perform for the opening evening.

Charlie was busy setting up, the 'Wheel of Fortune', as they were calling the game. It was made up with a wheel that spun around freely with black and red pockets along the interior wall for the metal ball to end up in when the wheel finally stopped rotating. Each pocket had a number too, so you could bet colors or numbers, odds and evens or any combinations. "Masso we got to get this piece of gaming equipment, it is a money maker. It has several ways to bet, but fewer ways to win," was Charlie's suggestion, so the group voted on it. This model had the deluxe feature, where the games operator could control, if the ball went red or black, odds or evens, so as to control losses or even abate wins.

Divain was out distributing invitations to the area men of importance, making the pitch. "This sir is a gentlemen's club, by invitation only, and may I present you a personal invitation."

 Albert Rizzio was now the operations manager. He was deep in his element, pulling the whole thing together and pushing it forward. He had hired the night crew and personally trained the bars help and the order talkers. This was a new idea Masso came up with. Free cheap drinks for men who were actively gambling, serviced by men who would move throughout the club, filling empty glasses of gamers. Security was also around inside and also in the parking area to break up fights, and keep the patrons safe from outside hijackers.

 The Big Money was set to open in just a few hours when over their morning meal. Rizzo once more went over the game plan. "Tonight is a practices run, I expect a few problems. So keep your heads up if you see something that needs adjusting bring it to my attention. There should be lots of cash will be moving through our hands tonight, and if we are successful, it will be a recurring venture."

 "Note," Masso pointed out. "A couple things, keep the cheap drinks flowing to the game players of Cee-Lo, the card games and of course our big draw, the wheel of fortune. Drunks make stupid mistakes. Second, we will let more money go out tonight than comes in. We want several big winners, and many more that leave with more than they came in with, even if it's only a few liras. Next weekend we will have set the hook and can start getting our money back. Last and most importantly, keep an eye out for the new Don of Del la Rosa. As I told you all before, he is only 5'3" tall and jet black hair. He is and I repeat, he is our true mark. I want him hooked on Cee-Lo, so he can think of nothing else when he is not here playing. Charlie when he does come in, you'll know how to play him. Slowly, just letting him win a little, he will come back again and again as long as he thinks he has the game figured out. Then in a couple of weeks, we will execute our plan. Any questions, no? With all said, I wish you all the best of luck tonight, and enjoy." Masso's himself would not be there tonight, for he wanted to stay out of the light and only come in when the final thrust was being played.

Early in the morning hours, after the club had closed and everyone but Rizzo had left, Masso joined him for the final report.

"The night was a bigger success than we could have ever expected, Masso, the cheap drinks kept everyone playing. The music acts and especially that magic guy, kept people entertained. He gave them something to do when not gaming or between games. Though please be aware, the entertainment can also cool them off too much as well. A few as you wished, actually went home with pockets full of cash, and many went home with a few more dollars than they came in with. Plus enough liquor was bought by non-players that it made up the losses and the tables themselves each did amazingly fantastic. "The Wheel" is, as Charlie pointed out, a golden egg laying big bird, laying huge golden eggs. I don't think your Don Del La Rosa came in tonight. I am sure his forman was here for a while, leaving with a few extra liras. So it should not be too long now that the bait has been set." These were Rizzo's final words, but before he left he pushed, across the new table, the paper with the figures of the night's, net, net... They surprised even Masso.

"Really, these are correct, you sure?"

Rizzo just nodded as he left the now dark and quite building, finding the only one up this early was the coffee shop owner, who had only left the club himself an hour earlier.

"Success breeds inspiration for more of the same," was Masso's message to the group at dinner that next night. "So let's open Friday nights as guest night. We will open to accompanied women, wives and girlfriends, or both if the member has the coronas to do so. I believe we can use less drink on the ladies and still get the same results, then leave the big pot gamming for Saturday nights and for a few elite men we will open a membership only back room. It will be for high stakes gambling, free drinks and food. A registration fee will be set up to purchase the key that unlocks the green door. Anyone have a question or any suggestions?"

"So are we going to run women upstairs?" was Charlie's first question.

"No, that is not what I want right now. If, we only run a high- end gaming and entertainment establishment, the women of the area and the church may not give us much heat. We would have to close down in no time if they thought we were bringing prostitutes in, to tempt the morals of their husband's or son's and stealing their souls. Beside, we want our clients spending hours and cash on gamming not ten minutes of pleasure then go home." Masso threw out a few more suggestions as did each of the others and by the end of dinner a new type of club was being developed, which had entertainment Fridays for mixed company and then Saturday nights geared more for just a man's taste and also only opened on Saturday nights was the access by key only, **'Green Doored Room'**.

By Wednesday morning, anyone within a day's travel knew of the "Big Money". The following Friday found a packed mixed crowed, ready to test their luck. The little Italian harmonica player was also the MC and was a big hit, titillating, suggestive but never quite going over the line. The magician used only women when a volunteer from the audience was needed for a trick. The band with a male tenor singer only played love songs and ones that were upbeat. Still another no show from the new Don of Del la Rosa, Biaggio Narcis. Then again his foreman came in alone again. He played a few rounds of the dice game Cee-Lo, losing several passes but finally hitting two in a row, and after which he left. The night's take was double the opening nights.

 Discontents and unhappy losers would be the biggest problem this night. At least until they met up with Rizzo's threat of his ax handle. Or an unexpected encounter with Gerome who at times during the evening was tossing the unruly trouble makers out two at a time out the back door. Each one had been given a warning after which more physically measures were used. A few were beaten to prevent them from trying to reentering the building and then tied on to their horse or carriage and then sent home. These quick trips out back, then the encounter of a blow or two quickly improved most of these men's attitudes. It was also meant as a forewarning message that was being sent out to the community.

 That Saturday night was filled with a different crowed, men who had been the week before and had spent hours working out their strategy, men who had heard of the new club and wanted to test their skills. Then there were those who were just looking to taste the experience.

 It was a young, bored man who wanted to blow off steam that Rizzo was in the middle of removing, when Rizzo bumped into

Biaggio Narisi. Biaggio was dressed tonight like he was going to an opera in Rome rather than gambling establishment in old Sicily. " Welcome, Sir, I'll be right with you," Rizzo then turned back to his problem in hand, " look here you little drunk, walk out here now on your own feet or you'll be leaving with a little help from Gerome here, and don't come back until you are old enough to shave and drink." Rizzo turned back around extending his hand. "Alberto Rizzo, proprietor here at the *'Molti Soldi'* what are you drinking? The first one is on the house. Your Excellency, Divain get this gentleman here whatever he is drinking."

"Thank you Albert, yes this is my first time here, not a first time in a casino though. It looks like you have an interesting looking place here. I also heard you even have a special room for no limit games."

"Yes, though it is a very limited access game room by invitation only. I'm sure what we have here in front will be challenging enough. Our wheel of chance can be played several ways, with the option of playing several bets all at the same time. Over there are several tables with card games to participate in. If you're vice leads towards dice there is a Cee-Lo game going hot and heavy over the other side of the bar, and…"

"How do I get an invite to go through green door?" The young Don asked.

"I don't think you could qualify young man. The few who have are very wealthy and have provided financial guarantees from their banks, so consider what you can afford."

"Do you know who I am? I think not, I am- Biaggio Narcisi. My family is one of the very oldest and wealthiest *Palermo* families. I am now the Don of Del La Rosa. My family could buy and sell this whole town a dozen times over. Can't afford it, 'ha,' I can buy anything I want, and I have a pocket full of cash that should be good enough to get an invitation."

"Everyone you see here in front of you tonight Don, well they all came with cash too. Truthfully, I don't know anything about the Narcisi family or if you are even who you say you are? Now if you want, you can have your banker contact our Bank. It is the Alceu n Alliance Commercial bank of *Catania*. You have heard of the Alceu family I am sure. If you still have all that *Mucho Denaro* , come Monday then put some of it in an escrow account. It can be draw on for however much you feel you can afford to game with. Now may I suggest you might like the action at the dice table, do you know the game Cee-Lo?"

 Biaggio did play the wheel for a while but he found it was not the challenge he was looking for, but the sound of clicking dice kept calling his name, and was where he spent most of his night. Charlie took over running the game as soon as he saw their mark talking to Rizzo. The outcome of each play had long ago been determined, Two fast small wins then one big loss, then one good size win followed by another small win, then three losses, two steps forward, three back, one forward, one back, then two more losses, followed by a big win followed by two losses. In the end the young Don was chasing a lira by losing two. Until the last hand where he was intentionally sent home with a small profit, but Biaggio also left with a confident feeling that he had the game figured out.

As Rizzo thanked him for his patronage, the Don's reply was, "Your bank will hear from mine in the next few days. Oh by the way, does the house have any limits on bets?"

"We will cover up to a half a million on any one hand, does that work for you?"

The next Friday evening Narcisi came with a young lady as his guest. He was almost obnoxious to the point that if he had been anyone else, they would have been asked to leave. He was ordering the staff around like he was some sort of royalty. The little man was pretending to be a great Don, while all along trying to impress the young woman of how important he was and to let the staff knows he was special. Everyone needed to know how special he was, how he was to be treated or put up with his verbal wrath.

He gave the young lady a small hand full of coins and left her to entertain herself while he went to played Cee-Lo, Charlie greeted him. "Good evening Don Narcisi, are you ready to give us a chance to win some of our money back tonight? Don't worry I'll hold the next opening for you."

The first hour Biaggio spent showing his date his worldly knowledge of gaming, helping her playing the wheel of fortune game. "You see cousin, this is not a game of finesse, but timing is the key and good luck. Which you obviously have, because you are here with me tonight right? This whole night we might say will be a learning experience for you." *He could have not been more sinister.* Rizzo thought while listening in to the young Dons conversation, and picking up on his truer meaning.

 She tried to understand but the whole time he was speaking she just nodded and then just dropped the metal ball where ever it fell out of her hand, always losing. "No Antonietta, more like this," as he carefully placed the ball in play. "See, I won again. It is really so simple even a child like you should be able to do it now watch once more."

The second hour the new Don was increasingly frustrated looking over at the corner every few minutes, where the action he longed for, was being played. Listening to the hoops of winners and here he was with his young cousin. Plus his growing frustration by his inability to participate in the dice game he had come to play. Each time he heard the clicking sound it would be like a little dig under his skin. Finally after waiting two hours and still no openings at the Cee-Lo table, his guest's whining was enough to send the young Don home frustrated and vindictive. The Don's young cousin, Antonietta Biaggio's, was his date for that Friday night. She was rescued from the young drunk who was being verbally and physically abusive by the quick thinking Rizzo. "Don Narcisi you're leaving so soon, please allow the house one more drink to make it up to you. A Don's special please Gerome for our young friend."

The drink was a special concoction Masso had come up with to deal with overtly drunks and general troublemakers who came from families that would not be happy having their family members beaten. Instead for them one shot of Masso's magic drink. Within minutes, the consumer is dead to the world, and not a problem to anyone except what to do with the unconscious body. The next day when they do reawake they remember very little but the blistering pounding in their heads, which lets them think that they must have had a great time. Now though, they will have to pay for it. In this man's case he had only made it three steps out the back door when his ankles first, then knees, and finally his waist gave out and he closed down like according into dead bulk weight. Unfortunately, his insides imploded also emptying all his body's gases, his bowels and bladder too.

"Oh my, he smells like he, did he …. Is… is he dead?" asked Miss Narcisi. As she faced her savior, "I do hope so. He told me what he planned to do to me when he got me back to the estate. He is really not a very nice man and I really don't want to ever to be alone with him again."

"He will not bother you tonight. In the meantime I will get him back to the estate, drop him off, and arrange to pick up your things as well. I have a safe place for you to stay, if that works for you? Then tomorrow I'll escort you back to the train station and make sure you get headed in the right direction."

"Oh, Mister Rizzo thank you so very, very much, I know my father will pay you well for your time and help."

"You can call me Alberto or Al, and it is not necessary to pay me. I do it just for the chance to share some time with such a beautiful, charming lady."

"Oh my, Alberto, you really think I am charming, not just a silly young girl?"

"You are silly and a bit naïve Antonietta, but you are not a young girl, but then too, not quite grown women either. So this time, why don't we just call you a young lady and tonight was a lessoned learned." Rizzo checked her into the Black Rose and left her in the capable hands of Roberto until the next morning.

The last thing Rizzo said before he helped her climb onboard the train that morning that was heading home. "Antonietta, it was nice to meet you, and until next time," he gave her hand a light kiss. "Would you please give this note to your father after you tell him of your experiences? Thank you young lady, and have a safe trip home."

When his daughter returned home and gave him her version of the experiences, plus the note from the proprietor of the gaming house, it was all the head of the Narcisi family needed. The following Monday the Narcisi family's bank with drew all of the guarantees on the young Don's line of credit including the one at Big Money.

The holidays came and for the first time some of the men went home to celebrate with their other families.

Gerome took off early to spend a few days at his new home, and Rizzo who had not seen his family in many years along with Charlie both went to family celebrations.

Divain came with Masso to break bread and to consume many other wonderful edible delights that Mella had been working on for over a week. Bird eggs smoked, bat wings fried, a stew of so many colors, textures, and flavors, it was impossible to know for sure what he was eating, but he knew at the end of the day with mouth stuffed, that this meal was every bit as good as his father's table was having and even better because he knew by the way Mella looked at Masso it was made with love.

The Monday night of December thirty first, was New Year's Eve. At seven the doors opened again at the Big Money. At eight forty-five a confident Don Narcisi walked into the casino knowing after tonight he would no longer have any financial problems. He had scraped up ten thousand dollars in cash to play with, and he had a plan, a sure thing.

"Good evening Don Narcisi I did not think we would see you so soon, with your sudden capital shortage, and all." Rizzo could not help himself.

"I have my invitation and cash, so I would not miss it. I feel very lucky tonight, yes very lucky."

"Well sir, let me unlock the door for you and I do wish the very best of luck, and happy New Year in case I miss you latter."

The interior of the room was tastefully done, hunter green walls with rich carved dark wood trim. The walls contained a few of Rizzo's personal paintings from the booty wagon, a large brass oil burning chandelier hanging over the ten person oval black walnut table. The heavy chairs also carved out of walnut and covered in cow hide with the hair still intact. This was a man's room, and it was set up for the business of servicing the needs of its male inhabitants. Each spot had a spot to put your drink, a silver cup full of wood matches, and another one for ashes. At one end of the room was a beautiful cast iron wood burning stove with fine brass fittings and accents. On the other end of the room were four large stuffed leather chairs with a small mahogany table next to each. Masso felt, if you lost or won it would be in at least a beautiful and comfortable space to do so.

"The game is Cee-Lo gentlemen and it is you against the house. My name is Masso and I will be your host to night, any questions? Fine then let the dice roll to see who will be first."

Five players plus Masso sat or stood around the table that night. Each man played what he thought was their best games, up down, up, up, down, down, down, so the night wore on. By eleven- thirty the play was down to just Masso the Don and one old lucky player. "What do you say we up the ante for each game," suggested Biaggio, "say four times normal? It's late and we have only a half an hour left."

The next hand put the old man out and he moved to one of the chairs in back, to watch how this evening was going to play out. The young Don played his game perfectly and had managed to keep his stake and add a couple extra thousand dollars. The last game came up and his first roll was a four and a one and a three, the houses was a pair of fives and a six. "The bet is to you Mr. Narcisi."

"I bet the house the max five hundred thousand, I am all in."

"Unfortunately, you have only the cash in front of you sir, and it is nowhere near that amount, so bet what you have in front of you or put up something really valuable. What do you have to cover this bet?"

"My property's leases should more than cover it I believe, will that work?" *The final move will be up to this young kid he thought to himself.*

 His reply did not come at once, but as if Masso was considering the offer, he took his time to answer. "I'll take your bet, but please sign your commitment note, I think I have one here. The name of the property is again?" and so the delay was put into motion.

The two new dice that Biaggio had removed from his shirt cuff and swapped out with the other two were now in play. Narcisi with the certainty of a gold find and a big smile on his face started the play. Just before he was to raise his leather cup, Masso dropped his hand over the top, "wait," he said, "you did not date the commitment." Again a delay, "fine it's all yours now." Just before Braggio could complete his play, commotion from the old man watching, drew all of their attention back to the other side of the room. It was just a spilt glass of whisky and much cussing.

The young Don, full of himself and knowing he had just beat the house out of a half a million dollars, turned back around and was smiling from ear to ear. The young Don reached for his payday. He lifted the leather cup with an elegant confidence. What was showing was not a pair of sixes he had expected. Not even the same loaded dice he had snuck in. What was before him was a two and another one, a dead man's hand. Braggio just stared at the five dice, now laying out for all to see.

"Let's see if my luck is better," and as Masso lifted his cup, below were a pair of sixes, a killer hand and the winner. "Bad luck for you today sir, but tomorrow is another day full of all kinds of opportunities, right?"

Braggio sat stunned. He knew he had been played, not sure how and knowing he could say nothing as well. Numb he walked out trying to figure out what went wrong.

"Good night Don Narcisi, Happy New Year to you and we will be seeing you soon I'm sure," was Rizzo's parting shot.

"Did you see the look on his face as he left here?" Rizzo was laughing so hard he could barely speak." When the old man dropped his drink on himself... And was raising hell, every ones attention moved to him... You swapped those two cups as sweet as bushing off a fly, and with your right hand still on top of his cup, just like before. When he turned back around and still had that pig leaving the trough smile on his face." Rizzo still had hard time breathing from all his laughter.

"It was nothing to the one he had when he turned that cup over and found his dice not there but ones that sunk his boat." Laughed the old man from the game, who had been Divain dressed up to look like an old man. His whole face went from ear to ear grin to a look like he had just eaten a shit sandwich. I bet that old cook Masso nutted had the same look, ha,ha,ha."

The celebration that night went into the early hours. "A toast to our most brilliant leader and the man who has made this all possible for us all," were Gerome's words. As each took their turns each became more outrageous.

Finally the boss spoke, "Tonight my friends we have successfully completed the first set of objectives. We have growing businesses to support each of us. We have a strong bank to help us grow our futures. Lastly my Don Leonardo can finally come home. Now here's to next year, our challenges will be greater yet, but we are in position to take them on and also be successful. For this group, working together can do almost anything we want, to the New Year and her endless opportunities."

"Now what?" asked Rizzo the next afternoon after the meal?

"Thursday Gerome and I will visit the EX-Don at Del La Rosa and I sent word already to Arturo to find a comfortable carriage for Don La Barba, and for them to be prepared to head this way as soon as they heard from Mella."

The early morning of that Thursday the two found the front gate at Del La Rosa locked tight for the first time in over nine decades that the La Barba family owned the estate. Two shot gun carrying men sat behind a small wood burning fire as additional security just inside the gate. The two just keep on riding past.

"I guess he thinks he is secure in his gilded cage?" Masso whispered to Gerome as they entered the groves from high above the estate. That night there was no moon light and it looked like it might rain while they worked his way down through Masso's precious trees. Just as he had done hundreds of times before, sometimes with the light to show the way, and many more times without any light. "See over there," as Masso whispered as he pointed to the one guard that was at the back kitchens door. I bet there's another one at the front door too." They slipped past him and headed to the garden. "Here behind this Cypress, see." Masso lifted the old wood peg and pushed the door open, "down this path my friend." Masso looked one more time to make sure they had not gotten spotted and then ducked in leading the way, with Gerome's hand on his shoulder they moved forward. "We climb these steps and I'll look inside quick." The room was empty, so Masso waved Gerome in. "We need to find if we can the original lease papers. Look over on and in the desk, while I look in the shelves." The shelves looked pretty much as he left them after he and the Padre cleared out most of the valuable books and maps. As Masso stood back looking he noticed an old family bible, which had not been there before, sitting on shelf all by itself. He reached up and as he pulled it out the paperwork he was looking for fell out. "Here it is Gerome, did you find anything else interesting on his desk?"

"Just a lot of bills, demand letters and old bank reports, this guy is up to his ass in debits Masso."

 From the other side of the hall they heard Braggio screaming at someone." If you can't do it right, don't do it at all, you dumb whelp bitch, how hard is it to suck a cock?" "Who are you and how did you get in here?" Braggio asked as he walked in and saw Gerome going through his desk.

"He is with me, "the voice answered the question from behind him. The man turned abruptly to face the all too haunting voice and his biggest fear. "We are here now, and from your extra outside help, you seemed to have been expecting us. I am here to collect the four hundred and eighty- eight thousand dollars you owe the casino. Or just sign this lease which you pledged for your last play. Whichever works best for you of course?"

From his coat pocket the young Don pulled out an old flint lock pistol and pointed first at Masso then Gerome, I don't know how you two got in, but I suggest you leave the same way or I'll..."

Masso interrupted him. "Have you ever shot at anyone Braggio, or even fired this particular weapon? Even under the best of circumstances it's a fifty -fifty chance it will fire at all. Then if it does fire, they tend to send the lead to the left or right. Which way does this weapon fire do you know? Of course if you are lucky enough to hit someone with the shot, the damage from such a low velocity pistol would bring very little damage and of course you realize the gun only fires once. If you should hit one of us the other will just kill you where you stand. So put the art piece down and realize you only really have a couple options. "

"You cheated me, and have been playing me all along, so no I am not giving you anything and there is nothing you can do." The young man in a quivering voice replied.

"An honest man cannot be cheated. Those dice that gave me my winning hand were brought into the play by you not me. If you had let lady luck play out, who knows what hand she could have, had given you? So it was your actions not mine that brought you to this time and place. In life you sometimes have to pay up. This is one of those times. As I was saying choices, you can sign this lease agreement, walk away broke but alive, or. "

Before Masso could finish his sentence the pistol went off, missing Masso's neck by inches but striking his left shoulder. The response came quick when from out his right shirt sleeve a tiny dirk blade flew out slicing the top of the boy's hand, more like a scratch than a deep slice. "So you have made the first choice, now the next one consider very carefully. You are probably beginning to feel a burning on your wounded hand. That's because the blade was dipped in a special concoction. The pain you are going to find will not only get worse, but also will spread, without this." Masso reached into his pocket pulling out a small bottle. "You will die. Did you know Braggio that for just a few pence a word one can get some of the greatest forgers to copy signatures? I know some of those people. They can do your signature just like the one you signed at the Big Money last week? These men can also write suicide notes just like this one here," Masso lays down such a note," it looks just like your handwriting don't you think?"

The young Don just barely made it to the desks chair, before he began gasping for air, trying to talk and at the same time ignoring the pen and contract that required his attention. "No," was all he got out before he began to convulse.

"Just as well," said Masso, "some people can't appreciate the truth or reality. Even your own family will not miss you. As you already know you have never been their favorite son."

"How bad are you hit" as Gerome ran over to his companion, who pulled aside his shirt's collar to view a serious flesh wound but nothing, life threatening. "Can you wait to make it home before your wound is attended too, or do we need to find you some help sooner?"

"Let's set him up, put the pen in his right hand and the death letter under it. Leave the mostly empty bottle turned on its side and we will take this lease with us."

People were banging on the locked library door, alerted by the gun shot. As the two left the same way they came, shutting the swinging wall panel, just before the library's door was forced open. What the cook and one of the guards were to find, was the Don of the manor quivering his last breathes. The story got out quickly. Braggio's last communication was the letter which was left to explain his actions. In it, he explained what he felt. "This is my only way out after losing everything." The empty bottle gave his cause of death and the scratch on the top of his hand was never given a thought. "The gun shot must have been his last desperate attention getter, what a stupid man," were the words of his cook. "I wonder if the next owner will need a cook?"

"What have you got yourself into this time my son? Hold still and let Mella's old eyes have a look." She went to work on his wound. "Ah, more flesh than damage, take a deep breath now let it out slowly." He had heard her say those same words many a time before but to delivering mothers to be. With only her delicate but firm fingers she worked the piece of metal free of its confinement. "Well here is your problem," as she drops the flattened piece of lead in to his hand. Now, no using your left arm for a ten full days, do you understand me? Then slowly start using it as best you can. In six weeks you should be back to your dangerous old self," the old women laughed at her boy's expense.

Masso spent the rehab time at the estate overseeing the much to be done work inside before the Dons returned. Masso roared. "I want the interior of this house to be cleaned from ceiling to floor and everything in-between." The vineyards also need attention but not until after the February harvest of Lemons. Mella came in with a crew of workers and took on the challenge. Finding help was no problem, as soon as the word Don Leonardo was coming home got out. Volunteers showed up ready to work. The basement of Father Stefano was emptied out and its contents put back where they had been before. The orchards had trees full of ripening fruit, but much work had to be done even before on piece could be gathered. All the years of dead wood and spoiled fruit had to be removed, and the high grass between the rows had to be cut. The trimming and pruning would have to wait this year until after the harvest.

The former Don, packed in ice was sent back to his family, gladly paid by one Tomasso Del la Rosa.

The last thing to be done before the move was to deal with Francis La Barbra who had been traveling the continent with his brothers in law's for the last six months, under the pretense of generating new business opportunities. Masso had the bankers Goldin's leave Francis this message. "Urgent issues have come up, need to see you promptly," was one of the notes Francis found along with dozens of others, from creditors whose bills have gone unpaid for months. "What in the hell is going on here, why were these bills not paid?" Francis was beside himself. The next morning at the early hour of eleven he was at the doors of Goldin Bank. "What is going on here Hector? I come back to find the whole trading office empty. I have mad demand notes from creditors, and you're bank statements show I have had no income from anywhere in the last several months. Have you SOB lost your minds since I left?" Francis exploded as soon as he came barging in the family's banker's office.

Waiting for the La Barba and Luccus trading company's president in an adjoining office was, his Uncle Don Arturo, Felix Goldin, and Tomasso Del La Rosa.

"You're late as usual Francis. The others have been here for hours, in here." The old banker opened the door into the waiting conference room. *I am not looking forward to the next half an hour,* the banker thought to himself. "This way and all your questions will be answered, I think."

"What's so secretive that you had me come…, what are you doing here Uncle Arturo? It's the Don, he is dead right?" The joy in his voice faded suddenly when he saw the last member of the group. "What's he doing here? I inherit everything. That is the law. This sperm accident gets zero and I'll make sure he wished he was…"

"Sit down Francis, the Don is not dead. I wish for your sake and mine he was, but he is alive and doing well under the circumstances. Let me formally introduce to you the La Barbra's family's Abortrador . A position your father set up before his faithless meeting. Mr. Tomasso Del La Rossa. Masso, this is the Dons only son Francis La Barba."

"Abortrador, what does that mean?" Francis screams as he begins to get a sinking feeling in his gut, "What did that crazy old man do now?"

"First your family has used Abortrador's for many generations, so as far as your concerns, it a set precedence. Second it was a very insightful move by your family and the position has allowed them to survive. That is exactly what Masso has done as Abortrador for the benefit of both sides of the La Barbra family. His main responsibilities are to make sure the family survives and to position it for future growth," explained the banker. "A few months ago, your uncle came to us, with Masso and the confirming signed documents. My brother Stefano had been there and personally witnessed the signing himself. Your father's foresight actions have saved your family. The particulars we can speak of latter. Now though, whatever Masso says, is as if it were the Don himself was saying it. Do you understand?" The old banker asked.

"No I don't understand, he," Francis points to the young warrior, "Is running everything? It can't be so, why would my father do this to me?"

"It does not matter what you think or want at this point." Masso finally speaks. "My job is to keep communications open between the different branches of the La Barba family, so that's what we are doing right now. You have been stealing from the company for a few years and you have been using the Don's personal assets to cover your loans, also a no no. Lastly you have killed the golden goose, by leasing the families' estate which was not yours to lease. All the creditors that have the Don's property as collateral have been notified that the loan's collateral is not yours to pledge. That any agreement they had with you would not be honored by the estate. As of now the Alceu and Alliance bank hold over twenty thousand of your personally signed notes that are due upon demand. The assets you currently have control of, consist of the empty offices of La Barbra n Associates trading company in *Palermo.* One warehouse and dock, which is empty except for a few tons of lemon waste that needs to be sold. This is all that is left of your family's businesses that you do have control over. So maybe you can get more money from the Luccus family, or perhaps you have a big cash stash somewhere hidden. If not then you will need at least a line of credit somewhere from someone because otherwise you are zeroed out. Despite your attempt to kill me, to publicly humiliate me and the fact that I do not like you, my job is to make things go forward as our Don would want it. We are going back in time to find an answer for you and for the family's companies that you were given the responsibility for. I have you way out, but first do you think you can come up with one hundred thousand dollars from anywhere?"

The crushed man just shook his head no, while softly moaning.

"I did not think so, but luck for you I have begun looking for a suitable wife for you, someone whose dower could give you a second chance."

"A wife, did you say, a wife?" this reply brought a weeping and uncontrollable laughter all the same time, "Me, a wife, no, no, that is not happening, me married, becoming a father. Who in their mind would pay that kind of money to marry me in the first place?" He giggles, now without rage.

"Actually I already have had some interest from a few families and maybe we will just hold a bidding game. Anyway it's your only choice unless you want to give up your inheritance and just crawl away? Also, your father is being taken home back to the estate where he will be more comfortable and well looked after. You should try to see him before he leaves. One of my men will accompany him and look after his safety and his wellbeing. In the meantime your cousin Arturo has been living in the family's house in Palermo he has been looking after the Don and representing the family socially, both being things that you seemed to ignored over the last several years."

Don Arturo and Masso left together to meet separately to discuss the new office and how busy they were now with real in the demand commodities like sulphur and lemons.

When the other two men left, Hector broke the rest of news. "You are not going to like hearing this last bit of news either. Francis you never went back to the Cheezo family to get them to sign a new lease for the mining property. Masso did, and he now holds the whole ground lease. He was only going to use the lease for the empty cave, to store fruit and bulk ship it out on rail, a pretty smart idea actually. Anyway, when he was visiting the site a few weeks ago, as luck would have it, an earth quake just happened. Then an explosive charge was set off deep in the belly of the mine. These events happened almost at the same moment. This combination caused an eruption deep down in the earth's core. Those actions together allowed huge openings deep in the ground to open up, releasing fresh hot liquid sulphur. It came bubbling up filling back up the entire mine plus half the yard." The old Banker said what the both were thinking. "You realize of course that this would have been your answer for all your money problems forever."

"I can't get a break and that cum stain of my old man's, everything he does or touches he turns into gold. Do you think he is really doing me a favor by marrying me off like a prize stud horse or something?"

"What other choice do you have really? Also be aware Masso has also brought back with him a group of his army buddies. In just a few months they have begun setting up an Alliance of Citrus growers. Just like the Don was trying to do before he was attacked. They may have just started, but several members are now under contract. For sure they are mostly just small orchards but their membership is very inviting. They are also including a type of protection insurance from thieves. The members also are being offered loans through a new bank which the Alliance also owns along with the Alceu family of *Catania*. They will be able to provide needed capital for members to expand or improve to their own orchards. The small and medium orchards would be crazy not to join, what would they have to lose? Next, Masso has also set you Uncle up with trading offices and a small dockside warehouse for La Barba and Son Trading in *Catania*. One of his boys is staying at the oldest warehouse on the main land, to oversee what's left of the business. Then your cousin, the Captain, you remember him? The one that was to make sure your nemesis was never to return. He himself returned as a civilian and is now working for the family in *Palermo*. Lastly the group and Masso opened a gambling casino in *Pizza Armerina*. That's how he got the Del La Rosa back, with her two signed leases with over 45 years left, meaning no income for you on that even when you become the Don. You got to admit though Francis. He has for sure brains, ambition and an ability to get done whatever he sets his mind to, just like your father and he has been successful."

"I got to figure something out, that Bastardo has got to make a mistake. When he does, I am going to be there. Then I'll just put him down, once and for all when it does happen. Listen to my words old man." Francis and the banker both knew those were just empty threats, at least right now.

The next few weeks were busy, after the Don got home, Mella moved back to the estate to personally take care of her old Parton. Masso energies now were directed back overseeing the estate's collection of the fruit as well as the several Alliances members harvest's as well. All in order to make sure he knew how many tons the La Barbra and Son's trading would have to sell.

One evening a neighbor of Masso's and a member of the Alliance came to him about a threat he gotten that morning.

"Don Del La Rosa, I was met in my field by a Ganza family's lemon buyer. He told me that next week he would have his pickers ready to harvest my trees. I explained that I had already made arrangements for this year's harvest and was in fact under a contract to the new Alliance of Citrus Growers. He told me that I could do whatever I want with that contract, but he was getting my harvest one way or another."

"I am glad you came to me my friend. The Alliance will take care of the situation, so don't worry. Now if something happens in the next couple days alert me. Go home and get ready for a great harvest." Over the rest of the day others that had signed up were also visited by these two men of the Ganza family. They too came by to express their concerns. The Ganza family had been running roughshod over the areas smaller growers for years.

The next morning Masso , Rizzo and Gerome met for an early morning breakfast at the Rose.

"I want you two to meet up with those two local Ganza bullies and explain to the one you don't leave hanging upside down in a tree, gutted, that our Alliances members are not to be threatened or contacted ever again. Or else!"

The message was sent, and the fact that these men were not just a bunch of thugs was noted by Don Ganza who was now going to have to deal with this new threat with a different approach.

Masso moved into what had been Mella's and Augusto's estate's small bungalow. So he could keep an eye on things first hand.

 "The big groves have contracted most of the picking help and Ganza has put the word out for no one to work for us or else. " Divain reported the news back to Masso, just a few days before the harvest was to begin.

"Call a meeting of all the members to meet at Black Rose for dinner tonight and ask Mrs. O' Malley to fix something for a typical Sicilian family's gathering. Second, reach out to some other labor markets, picking fruit is not hard to learn. Lastly bring out of hiding the cannon and some rifles and ammunition just in case."

The next night Masso had gathered six heads of families that were part of the Alliance, and his men for a strategy meeting. "Gentlemen thank you for sharing bread with us tonight, I think this is a good idea for us to meet occasionally, outside the fields and share problems and ideas. We will either all grow together or dry up together as a group. We are currently looking for extra help, some of which might need some instruction but will have willing and able backs and hands. I also think we should all work each other's family's orchard's, as a group. That way we know everyone will still get his harvest completed. As a group we are starting to make a statement, people are noticing, watching. As we succeed, more farms will want to join us and the stronger we will be given more respected and feared if need be. So who's willing to try the idea?"

All six of the members plus Masso's guys all signed on to work each other's orchards.

Mella had to hire a few new people to fill in as staff for Del La Rosa. One was a beautiful young lady who helped in the kitchen. Her name was Carmel.

Masso found her naked in his bed a few nights after she began working. "Mella said I could sleep in any bed I wanted. This is the one I chose."

"Well then, I'll let you have it, I'll move back into the barn." Masso turned to leave when she pulled back the covers exposing herself.

"It's cold in the barn. Would you not rather share this one?" He was still a man even if he did not have much experience with women or girls but his brain between is ears turned off and his other brain took over.

 Early the next morning mother and son meet briefly in passing. "Your bed mate last night, was she satisfactory to you, my son?" Asked Mella , with a wicked smile.

"Was that your idea or hers?" He asked.

"Does it really matter? You are a man, Men have needs and strong men have very strong needs. Your old mother knows these things so enjoy."

"Her idea or yours? " He asked for the second time, "It is important, or I would not have asked."

"Well she asked about you, and seemed interested so I just suggested she meet you after work. She took the initiative, personally I admire her taste. She reminds me of myself at that age. That's how I ended up here you know a lover to an older powerful man."

He did not turn her away and over the next few weeks they spent most nights in passion, when he was home. A quite relationship was begun if only to satisfy each of their youthful curiosity and passions.

The last of March found the last lemon picked and on its way to *Catania*. Masso was glad the worst of this year's problems with the harvesting was in the past and now he would have a proven record to show as he went about enlisting new members to the Alliance. He approached his cabin that night he felt relief and had not one care in the world for the first time in a long time. Within the home he heard voices he was not familiar with, but the tone of conversation did not send any warning signals. Masso cautiously opened the door. Inside at the table sitting was Carmelo, behind her a man holding a knife over her, another came from behind the door was carrying a Lupara. The third man was holding a pistol and stood across the table from Carmelo. "Please step in Mr. Del La Rosa and join us." The man behind Carmelo was talking. "We have just been having a nice little talk with you pregnant, *cummari* here. She told us you just finished your harvest, which is perfect. All I need for you to do, is simply turn over all this year's harvest to Don Ganza . You just sign this, and we will be gone." The man with the revolver stepped up behind him and laid some paperwork in front of him next to an ink well and pen. "Just sign here and we will leave you two to your business, "he laughed. "Or we will kill her then you, so sign up."

 Masso bent down to look at the document and slowly picked up the pen, without a second thought he grabbed the man's right hand that had the pistol, and with his own right hand stuck the pen through the man's ear, deep into his brain, and with the revolver now in his control, lifted the man's arm and fired directly at the holder of the knife. The only sound Masso remembers was the screaming from Carmel, "Noooo," as she stood up as if to protect the man behind her. It was too little, too late. The bullet passed through her first then buried deep into the man behind her. The last man was now on the floor babbling and certainly not a threat. Masso went around back and found the wagon they came in tied up. He quickly loaded all the dead bodies. He felt nothing. The exception was when he put Carmelo's body in the back of the wagon. Gently he laid her down. "You were a just a little girl, put in as a pawn piece. I don't know if you even knew it, but in the end, you choose the wrong side in this war." He then loaded the crazy man up in the driver's seat and sent them all back to where they had come from.

At the next morning meeting at the Black Rose, Masso went over the night's events. "The funerals will be in a few days. Only after they are in the ground will Ganza send a force. We will be ready for them. Set up the cannon on the hill at four corners and set up cross rifle positions on two of the other points."

 Just like the boss had predicted, the day after the funeral. Ganza sent seventeen heavily armed men out, with these simple instructions, "You can kill any one you want, but I want that boy for myself. He will regret killing my precious Carmelo, she was so sweet and only fifteen. He seduced my innocent nice. That Bastardo put his seed in her then killed her like an unwanted bitch dog. Go ahead and wipe out those upstarts. Above all though capture the man who killed our family members. I have plans for that boy. Slowly he will suffer under my own hands, before I personally kill him."

The riders came in full rush. Tightly grouped together, the first shot of the cannon took out seven men and five horses. The rifle men took out another five riders. All this happened before the group knew what was happening. Two more were shot in the back as they turned around and were running away. The three who escaped were so badly shaken it took almost an hour to get the full story out. The Don had no other plans and only regrets. When the remainder of the family got back from the second mass funeral, they found Don Ganza in the barn with a gunshot wound to the head. It looked like a suicide, but no one knew for sure.

 The Alliance had made a statement to the area, and Masso's had earned the fear and respect that his Patron had discussed with him so long ago.

Masso's first trip out on the road after the harvest was to the Delfino estate to arrange a group meeting of Lucia's neighbors. She held contracts for their lemon. He could tell something was wrong the moment he rode onto the estate. The trees had been harvested but it looked more like they had been ravaged by a storm not by skilled pickers.

"Oh Masso, I am so glad to see you. She has been kidnaped, they want …and I don't know where to go and get, and." Then the young man began to cry. This was what he was greeted with, from a panicked Enrico.

"Ok slow down, and start from the beginning, who was taken and by whom?" Masso was now on alert.

"I told her not to double cross the Calderone's. That old man is crazy, I'm telling you."

"So you're telling me the Calderone family kidnapped your sister Lucia, and now they want cash for her return?" Masso asked.

"She allowed them to take our harvest, but refused to turn over her contracts for the other orchards she holds. She was picked up last week and this letter was left in her place." Enrico's hand was shaking as he handed over the demand note.

"Why did you not reach out to me last week? Masso read the note twice and then handed it back to him. They wanted all the money that Lucia was getting for those contracts as the ransom. "What's the problem? You should have received the moneys from this year's harvest by now, so pay them."

"I can't, father arranged for only Lucia to have access to the accounts. Even if I could go to court but that could take months, or year. I told Agosto all of this. I got a package from them this morning it was Lucia's ear, they cut off her ear, her ear, my God Masso what am I going to do?"

Over the next hour Masso grilled Enrico all about the Calderone family. "Let's start with a few basic questions, how many men worked for them?"

"I see usually the same four guys'. They work mostly in the orchards and livestock. But who knows how many others the family employs. The residence has a couple women in the house, cooks and such, but why do you need this information?" Enrico now started to get a bit worked up again. The only part of their estate I have not been to is the old man Calderon's prize pig operation. He raises these special high dollar pigs. The whole operation is off limits to everyone. Only he tends to them."

"Ok, I'll ask the questions you just answer as best you can. Tell me, all about the family members, about the estate's lay out and every detail." He tried to squeeze from Enrico brain every little bit of information, even if it did not seem important. "You have seen his operation, have you any idea where they may be holding her?"

"I don't know for sure, like I said, the only area I have not been is Don Calderone pig farm. No one is allowed up there. He is a scary man and sometimes I don't think he is right in the head Masso."

"Keep communicating with them, and let Agosto know you are working on getting a loan on the estate, but it may take a week or so, and any more pieces of your sister removed will only delay the payment. In the meantime let me see what I can do, to deal with the situation."

He hurried back to Piazza Armerina and gathered his crew for a group session. "I think I have a plan that should work, Charlie, pull Don's La Barbra's carriage out, and get it cleaned up spotless. Then have the sign painter paint some royal coat of arms on the sides. Ask the groom in the stables to clean up the Dapper Gray Make her look like she was going to a wedding. Divian go to town, and get some clothes fitting a rich gentleman out for a ride, and Gerome you need to get some clothes that look like you are the royal's carriage driver. Rizzo ask around and find as much as you can about the famous pig farmer, Don Calderone."

On their weekly Sunday walk the Mistress of the estate Donna Vizzni, Calderone, Don Carmine's wife, and his daughter Grazia, were to see off in the distance a royal looking carriage coming toward them.

"Could that be my Duke Jamila coming for me finally,"Grazia pulled her right hand over her brow, in order to shad the sun light from her eyes, and to allow her a better view?

"Stop, with your fantasies Grazia, no royal man is coming for you and certainly not today. It was a long time ago and you need to move on with reality." Her mother quickly reprimanded her.

 "Royalty donot lie mother and he has come to claim me as he so long ago promised. I can just feel it, how do I look?"

 The carriage slowed down as it approached the two standing by the road. When it came upon them the driver stopped. Then a very handsome blond man stuck his head out of the window.

He does not exactly look like she remembered but it has been years since we last met, so maybe he has changed, Grazia thought to herself.

"Good morning ladies, Oh Grazia, you have grown more beautiful than I remembered. Is this your sister? I am Duke Jamila, Madame. I have come to make good on my promise to your family. You have not married anyone else, my love, have you? No, I can see your hand free of any gold bands."

"I am Grazia's mother, Lady Donna Vizzini Calderone, and why are you really here Duke, whoever?"

 The driver had gotten down and opened the door for the two ladies, extending his arm like he had been doing this for centuries. "Please ladies, join me and I will be happy to discuss my plans and purpose for this visit. We must have some champagne while we talk, and I don't really want to discuss anything here in the middle of the road. Please join me. Let us celebrate our join good luck. Gerome," the Duke commanded.

The two ladies looked at each other, then Grazia almost jumped into the carriage with one jump, her mother was more graceful and elegantly. She stepped up each stair with both feet on the same step, before moving to the next step. She then, grabbed the young mans extended hand and sat down across from the two young lovers. She knew that Grazia had given her virginity to this man years ago, and in doing so pitied away her only one asset. *Maybe this is a miracle after all*, the old women thought to herself. As the group chatted on, the women did not notice where they were going and when champagne was offered the two women eagerly consumed several glasses. It was not long before the sleeping ingredient put in was to take effect on the two women and the rest of trip back to Mella's empty old lakeside house went uneventful.

"Ladies I am sorry for our little ruse. We will try to make your stay as comfortable as possible, as long as you cooperate. We are trying to work out your release as soon as possible. Now in order to do so I need a few things. First I will need each of yours earrings please." Gerome asked gently but firmly.

The headaches they both had when they came to was nothing to the embarrassment they were feeling for falling for the whole royalty thing. "I knew something was not right, it was all too easy,too unreal. Like some Duke who you let take your virginity ten years ago was coming back. You my dear gave your only asset, and what for. A mere promise he was going to come back and make good. We both have been fooling ourselves Grazia. We have been living that lie way too long," were Lady Donna's first words to her daughter when they awoke and found themselves in this dark forbidden room, which smelled like a pasture?

Again Gerome asked, this time with more urgency. "If you ladies would be so kind to remove your ear rings, I will get you something for your headaches." Gerome always trying to be the gentleman first.

 "You can't have my earrings. They are a family treasure." Madam Donna, told Gerome.

"The choice is yours of course," Gerome said, "you give them to me, both of you now. Or I will be forced to use my own method, before we send them back to the estate with your ears attached. Just like your husband did to Lucia Delfino's family just a few days ago, your choice?" As the large man pulled out a meat slicing blade, "Now ladies what will it be?" Then as he reached down to touch Garzia's neck, she started screaming, "You can scream as loud as you want and for as long as you will, there is not a living soul within ten miles of here.

The two ladies hurriedly took off their earrings and turned them over to the big man who seemed to be in charge. "Thank you for making it easier on all of us, this is not the way we do business but hopefully it will not take too long to resolve this stand off and every one can go back to their lives. You can speed this up if either one of you might know where the Don might be keeping Miss Delfino?" He got no response as he really expected.

The screams did bring in Grazia's prince charming though. "Ladies would you care for some clean water, or something to eat?" Divain asked, as he brought in a basket full of fruit, fresh bread and cheese along with a bucket of freshly drawn water.

"I need to relieve myself. Are you going to let me up?" The old lady asked.

"Me too," Grazia spoke up. Are you going to watch us?" she asked as they came to the small outhouse.

"I am not a pervert Miss. My mother raised me better than that. But if you try to run away, we will take means to prevent that from happening. Do you think your father is treating Lucia this well? I doubt it, so just go in and take care of your business. I will be just down the hill there."

"He is right you know, your father probably has terrorized that poor girl and cutting her ear off, so sounds like him."

"Do you really think he cut that girls ear off?"

"Come on ladies you don't need all day to do whatever you need to do." Came the voice of that handsome man who had already gotten the attention of Grazia. "You know mother, he is really more beautiful than that Duke and under the circumstances he has been quite kind, don't you think?" Grazia whispered.

The Don Calderone arrived home that night expecting a full meal to be ready on the table. Instead the house was dark and quite. "What the hell is going on here, where are your sister and mother?" He asked Agosto when he too came in looking for Sunday dinner. All they found as they came into the dining room was the box and note addressed to Don Calderone. The Don quickly opened the note first fearing what might be in the box. The note confirmed what he suspected. They had been picked up and the cost was to be the return of the Delfino girl and a large sum of cash.

 Agosto ripped open the box while his father was reading, inside two set of familiar earrings.

"They have mother and Grazia those sons -of -bitch devils. Wait until I get my hands on that little weasel Enrico. He will wish he was dead. Let's go get them now."

"This was not done by Enrico he does not have the ability to do this and I doubt even if we found him he would even know where they are. They are safe for now. If they had sent the ear bobs back attached to the ears then I would worry. These guys are weak. We can use that to outsmart them. Go into the kitchen and bring us something to eat while I think about this." As they ate Carmine talked out loud about what he knew and what he surmised. "If it was not the Delfino boy I bet it was that Bastardo of Don La Barbra's. I heard he was back and causing problems for Don Narcisi and beat that little sex pervert from Palermo out of his property too. I think I have a plan to kill a present and a future problem all at once."

Over the next couple of days the negotiations took place, and each party thought they had the upper hand. Finally the time, place and amount was reached.

The Sunday exchange was in a park almost at a midway point. It was not a very busy this time of year so the only people that were meant to be there would be there. No sudden surprise visitors. Each side was to only have one driver and one negotiator. Gerome and Divain brought the two ladies in the carriage early hoping to see if the other two brought more people than agreed. The two men who brought Lucia in the wagon were not Carmino or Agosto and Lucia was facing backwards hiding her face. As soon as both of the parities got close enough to see each other and be heard, the conversation began.

"Are you two all right Madame Donna", the driver asked? "Yes we both are quite well," she answered.

Gerome in turn asked, Lucia. "Miss Delfino, how are you doing? No verbal reply but just a raised hand.

From the tree above where the carriage stopped. Agosto dropped down on the roof. He was to shoot the driver first then the other man, but when he looked up the big one was gone, and so he swung down to enter the carriage, gun hand first. "No Agosto," yelled Garzia, as she grabbed his hand, "You are ruining everything."

Divain was out of the cabin even before the hand with the gun entered, and he rolled back under the carriage, coming up next to the man who came to kill him, the same man whose gun arm was being held tight by his own sister. With no thought other than to execute Masso's plan, he slit the assassin's throat.

As Gerome rolled out from his position in the seat to the ground, he thought to himself, 'Masso was right again.' From behind his coat he swung out two Luppa's one for each hand and as the two figures in the wagon stood up they were blown out of the wagon by Gerome's shot guns blast.

"Are you ladies all right?" Divain asked? "Grazia you saved my life. I don't know what to say except thank you."

As she let go of her brother hand, she looked up at him then said, "You could marry me."

"Ok ", he replied.

Deep in a corner of the estate was Carmino's prize pig farm, with a small house where he often stayed the night or even days at a time and it was known by all on the estate to be off limits to everyone. It was here that Masso went looking for Lucia. He had walked as close as he could last night to get to know the space. This morning as he creped around the back of the barn he caught movement within and heard a sow squealing like she was being killed. What he viewed made him sick. He had heard rumor but there in front of him was this grown man with his pants off and mounting this poor animal. Masso turned and went around the other side of the pen where the Don's prize boar was in an extremely agitated state, rooting up everything and angrily looking for a way to get out. A simple pull of a latch and the four hundred pound eating machine was loose. Within seconds the sharp tusked animal had his mouth around the man naked butt and he was tossing him like a rag doll. Before he could do anything the pig had his face in his mouth, the teeth of the hog crunching down despite all the screaming which stopped abruptly after the second munch.

"Lucia are you here? Yell out if you can." From within the house was a moan. Inside tied to an old wooden chair Masso found

Lucia, alive but not well. "It is all over now and it's time for us to go home, can you walk?"

"Yes, but what just happened outside? It sounded like you killed that sick pervert in some crazy way and by the sound of it painfully, is he dead?" Lucia was if nothing else a full blooded Sicilian and revenge was as sweet a feeling as a cold glass of water on a hot day, both greatly appreciated and needed.

"Come out and see for yourself then we must go before someone notices you're gone."

In the barn both of the pigs were finishing what was left of the eatable parts of the former Don.

Masso took Lucia to Del La Rosa first for Mella to look after her. He then headed back to the Big Money to see if Rizzo had heard from the other two. When he got there a celebration of sorts was being held."

"Well you're back, alive, and happy so what happened?" asked Masso?

"Well it went pretty much as you expected. They came without the girl, and thought a one- man surprise attack on us would allow them to overpower us and take back the two women. What they did not expect was the charm power of Divian. Grazia was the one who warned Divian and actually held her brother arm preventing from shooting his target. While Divain escaped under the carriage in order to killed Agosto, all the while Miss Calderone held on tight to her brother's arm. By the way Divian and Grazia are engaged, that is if you give the go ahead. So that's what we are here celebrating," Gerome explained. "The ladies are at the Black

Rose with Roberto looking after them. Did you find the Delfino girl. Was she still alive?"

"Yes and if I never see what I saw today ever again, it will be alright with me. I left Lucia with my mom and when I tell you the whole story you are not going believe me." In his own story telling way Masso gave a vivid description of what he saw and heard." That boar was madder than anything I had witnessed before, and I watched him get his revenge."

Divain came up to Masso when things quieted down. "It just kind of happen, I was thanking her for basically choosing me over her own brother. I told her I owed her my life. Then she said, "Ok, then marry me," and I said, "OK, it just sort of felt right."

"If you really want to marry this woman, and become a farmer then, I will see what kind of marriage contract I can work out for you. If you are happy, then this might be a good thing for you and all of us Don Divian, as long as you join the Alliance." He joked but in a serious way. That is if you still want to marry her, if not that will be your problem not mines."

That evening Masso checked in on Lucia. He found the two women outside, making soap in a large black caldron that Mella had used for ever. What he saw when he rode in was the firer spreading up the sides of the iron pot, illuminating to two figures. "Well ladies, it's good to see you're both busy at work. Lucia, I am so glad to see you up and being yourself. I told Enrico it may be a few days or more before you would be ready to come home. Do you ladies need anything?"

"Yes my boy, Lucia is a real Sicilian woman, it will take more than one immoral, devil to get the best of her. She needs to be around another woman now, but she will be a stronger person for what she has been through, just giver some space." Mella tried to reassure him with what he knew already.

"Before you go, I want to thank you. You always seem to show up when I need more than just a friend, more like my guardian angel, which also carries a sword. Thank you again, and…" it was about time when Lucia finally broke down and began crying, short breathes and sobs at first, but with heaving weeping follow shortly."

 "Go my son, we will be all right."

His next stop for the night was to meet with Madame Calderone. "I am sorry the events of the last few days had to happen and had to involve you and your daughter, but as you know by now your husband began this conflict. What has passed cannot be changed, on the other hand when God takes away with the left hand he gives back with the right one, yes? It seems your daughter wants to marry my associate Divian. As his friend, he has asked me to work out the details of the wedding contract, if that is acceptable to you and your family?"

"Don Del La Rosa, left me say before we begin, Carmino Calderone was a mean spirited human, who loved his animals more than anything or anyone. He had been a hunting guide that by luck saved my father's life on a hunt. When my father asked him what he wanted as a reward, he asked for my hand in marriage. I was a prize. I had no more say than one of his pigs in who I was to marry or have children with. The death of Carmino by one of his own pigs is justice. As far as my son is concerned he was already a lost soul. He enjoyed inflicting pain on others just for his own pleasure. That poor Delfino girl, she was just like me. She was brought into something she had no control of, or desire to be a part of. How is she Masso? Carmine had not reason to disfigure her like he did."

"Lucia is a very strong woman, like you, and she will take this as a learning lesson that life has given her, and will come out in the end, even a stronger woman. I will let her know your concern for her wellbeing."

"Now your friend Divain, we have gotten to know him over the last few days. He has made every effort to make our confinement as pleasant as possible, under the circumstances. He is an educated man, who has been raised well, and who my daughter has fallen in love with. We Calderone women know what we want and will fight for it with all or heart. Grazia choose him over her own brother when the decision needed to be made. So with that being said, the truth is now the Vizzini orchards have no leader, no Don. The Vizzini estate has been in my family for over a century, and has only had men to run the day-to-day and handle everything. So we will now need a strong leader to take her over and make the estate grow the finest lemons in this valley as we had done in the past. I would hope with your help, to convince Divain,to be that person."

The next two hours Masso negotiated with one of the best he had ever gone up against. The Vizzini family estate was to get a new Don, one with different goal. Members of Donna's Vizzini family which her husband ran off would be allowed back to the estate, to help manage the large orchards. The estate would join the Alliance, to handle the sale and security, of all fruit the property grew. A large cash settlement was to be made to Lucia for her trauma and loss of her ear. Lastly the pigs were no longer to be a part of the family's business.

Divian was as happy as a kid at Christmas. He was to be the Don, a position even his own father could not provide for him. He also could see the huge potential for profits that Masso had negotiated for him.

It had cost Lucia her ear, but she was now the Defino's Don if not in name in at least real power. No one would ever doubt her word again. Once she forgave her brother and put him on a short tether, life went back to normal. She was pleasantly surprised though when Masso came by and gave her the message from Madame Antonietta. A bank draft had been sent with the apology letter.

"Well my friend you have saved my life, my estate and taken care of my enemies."

"Well your welcome. The last few months have really put the Alliance through a series of test. The guys are professionals and were just what was needed. "

 "Masso, do you realize how an amazing person your mother is? She is such a caring person and made me feel so much better. We talked a lot, about you some, but more about being a strong women in a man's world. She is the first woman I have been able to speak freely with since my mother died. You and Don La Barbra are so lucky to have some like her to love you. Thank you again. Anything you need from me is yours."

At the evening meal all five men plus Roberto, who seemed to have been adopted into the group, sat around the table to discuss Divan's up and coming wedding.

"Well my brother's, let's drink to the first of us to be wed. All for just a little love tunnel regularly and for the small country he will soon be Don over." As would be expected it was Charlie who would be the first to start the graphic, and salacious words for the evening.

As the dinner ended Masso stood up, "If I might have one more bit of your time gentleman. Rizzo and I have been getting request for security details for some of the biggest estates on this island, even a few the mother church seems own and are also some of the most productive orchards around. I want to cover as many of this request as possible. So reach back out to the people you think will be trainable, and will be loyal. We will set up a training camp like we did in the army, maybe not so in-depth but basics and that way we can see what each of these men are made of and which ones would bend under pressure."

Late in the night when only Rizzo and Masso were left the real plan was revealed. "So how many men do you think we are going to need, Masso?"

"A couple hundred maybe more, not all at once, we don't want to seem like we are forming our own army to take over the whole country, but that is exactly what we are going to do."

"Really, why so many?" Rizzo scratched his head.

"Securing the land for rich and for the out of country landowners is fine. It will give us an opening to control their produce as well, but there is an even bigger market out here. Every port on this island needs us. The amount of theft is staggering. Our services will be paid for by the savings we can offer the warehouses and docks."

"Masso , you are right, and if there was to be product lost by theft, it should be us doing the stealing, brilliant. That's why I love you man- you are always two steps ahead of everyone else."

"Rizzo, what do you know about the Tin Men?"

"Just the old saying, **if the tin man comes to town without a cup to sell, then someone is dead already.** Why do you ask?"

"We will need some men with their expertise in the future, and I don't want any of us to be too close to those jobs. I got lead where to go to arrange a meeting. I think it will be a good use of my time to follow up on it."

The next morning Masso left for the Waterfall of the Devil or Cascata-del-Diavulu. The final approach by road was though a vast and thick old growth forest which let in very little light. As Masso passed though he could not help but have a feeling of forbearance.

 The sound of the water roaring was heard long before he got close enough to see it. Then when he came out of the trees he found a most breathing taking of sites. *This must be the place Mother Nature has done some of her most amazing works*, he thought to himself. In front of him the source of the deafening noise. The melted snow swept down from high in the mountains which created the river before him. Looking at it from here the river was like a torrid flow of angry white and silver water which separated the valley he was coming from, and the base of the mountain range that was his destination. In front of him the water continued to drop downward with the fury of a thousand wild horses, flying over the rocks and boulders then disappearing in a cascade over another much deeper drop.

Close to the water's edge Masso found the old inn and his first stop.

"Good day sir, what can I get you this afternoon?" A beautiful young waitress, asked as he sat down in the inn's patio.

"Today's special and a pot of boiling water. May I ask you a question, is it always so noisy?"

She gave him a bright smile and with a so slight, laugh. "Actually you have arrived at the optimum time. Most of the year it is just a slow flow, or nothing at all, like in the middle of the summer. The spring melts always bring the most spectacular views."

There was something about her that struck a stirring deep inside him. Maybe it was her two tone green and gold eyes. They were like nothing he had ever seen on anyone else. They seemed so familiar and comforting at the same time.

He spent a few hours just taking in the views of both the water and this young woman. When she came back after he finished his meal she asked, "is there anything else I can do for you sir?"

"I want to visit the village of Tin Smiths which I understand are around here. Do you know the way?"

"There are only two ways there, but I will get my uncle to speak and advise you, wait right here."

Shortly a heavy round man came up to Masso's table and introduced himself as the Inn's proprietor, "My niece says you wish to go up into the mountain to visit the craftsmen. We have many items that they make right here inside, have you looked? We might have what you are looking for right here."

"Thank you sir, but is not tin wear I am after, a different type of business I seek. I heard that there is only two ways in and out, is it true?"

"This time of year the path across that bridge over there and up the narrow path is the only safe way, and it is too late in the day to start today and tomorrow the path is open only for villagers to come down no one can go up until the day after. May I ask have you been invited by any of them? If not, it is not a safe place just to sight see. The locals are very leery of strangers."

"The other route is it any more difficult? Why should I not try that way?"

Yes the other way is open, but it is much longer and requires crossing the tops of these mountains. It is spring time but winter storms still can come across these rock fortresses, and if you're not prepared , well, you could easily die. Are you sure your business is all that important to risk your life on it?"

"Thank you sir you have given me the answer I sleeked."

Masso left, still feeling he was missing something, but moved on after he decided to take the mountain top approach. Hoping to get a good way up the mountain and to find a camp site before sunset. The climb was easy at first but the further up the incline grew steeper. *I can see what the Inn keeper meant, if a fast-moving winter storm were to come through here. While I was in the middle of the climb, there would be little protection from its furry*. Masso pondered, but as he rounded the next corner he found a small flat area that would be suitable for a nights rest. As he looked around for any firewood, he noticed a small trickle of water running across the ground. *This may be the secret path*, Masso said to himself. The one he had heard about while listening to his Patron telling Father Stephano about his latest journey. It had happened many years ago when they though he was asleep. Letting his curiosity get the better of him Masso followed the water to its source up the path, and behind the large rock which was hiding what he had been hoping to find, a cave. The hole in the mountain looked like it went directly through the mountain he was about to cross. *"This is the short cut I bet,"* he said to no one.

Masso came back and gathered his things back up. He began walking into the big black hole, just inside against the wall were several oil lamps, and after checking out which one had the most oil lite it and began the last part of his journey by following the well-worn floor deeper into the mountain cave. The trail was not straight or flat, but it did seem to be going in the right direction and parts did require climbing steps that had been chiseled into the granite. It still took Masso over two hours to get to the end and there he found one simple wood door. He knocked but no one answered, so he lifted the handle and putting the lite light first, and then moved through himself. What he found was the inside of a small room with one window that looked out on to the town and another door which led out to the towns square, but locked from the outside. *I could climb out the window*, he thought, *but then again a stranger walking around the area in the dark, may not be my best choice either*. So he set up his bed roll and lay down to sleep. The next morning when he awoke the door was wide open and as Masso ventured through the door he was greeted, not as he had expected but still greeted.

"I wondered how long it would take you to find out and come looking for answers. You are Don Leonardo La Barba's Bastardo are you not?" the voice came from a front porch of the dwelling next door.

"Don La Barbra is my Parton sir, yes, but I had not come to seek answerers but services. What did you mean looking for answers and how do you know my Don?"

"Masso, is it not? Please join me for a coffee and let us talk." The speaker was about his Don's age and built like the proprietor of the inn far below.

"My name is Jaco, and you're Don and I go way back to when we were both young boys. I hate to say over fifty years I have known him. I wander off subject. He trained alongside us for two years and was a fierce competitor. But off point again, it was here he met your mother, she was just a young girl herself,but young love knows no age. Now where to start? Yes, his father had lost a bet and to fulfill the obligation he sent Leo. He was a bright student and fearless, but he did not really have the heart to do what needed to be done when it came time to prove his tin as we say. Try as he would he could not even kill a chicken, so he was rejected to join the tribe in the end, and he became the great Don he is today."

"Tribe," Masso questioned, "what tribe?"

"Our people are ancient warriors. Originally from an area around the Black Sea at least until the Mohmand's moved in and we had to flee. The tribe ended here in this valley between these three great mountain ranges. It was the closest thing to an invasion-proof place to live as the ancients could find. So now we thrived. We learned the tin trade and continued our warrior training. Some of our young men have traveled the world to fight enemies they were paid to kill. Paid in silver and gold coins for empires you never heard of. They would come back with riches, and stories of great battles and personal glories, and most importantly they brought back knowledge of different fighting styles they had learned. Styles they had to fight against. Our warriors are in a big demand, more demands than the bodies to fill them."

"I came myself to hire a few good men actually, we have begun to spread our influence, and when you take something of value from the rich and powerful they usually don't give it up easily, so I too am building an army.

"Excellent, you will stay a few days. Get to know your people and how we live. Maybe give a few lessons, and then you can see if any of your cousins will fit your needs."

"Jaco, is my mother here?" the young man asked , almost afraid of the answer, *what are, what will, her feeling towards me be like, and…* Thoughts were going through his head.

"No, after she gave birth to you her contract obligation was done and with the generous bonus Leo gave her she went to America. No one has heard from her since, I have often wondered how and what she is doing, she was my favorite sister's only child."

A relief settled over Masso, *well at least that will not be a confutation i will have to deal with right now*, he thought to himself. Finally his curiosity won out. "How did that whole thing work, if might ask?"

"In order to have warriors we need young men to train. Every family is required to provide one male child to the tribe to be trained not all will be up to the task, but they still have to try. The families with only girls must provide at least one of them to marry our warriors to supply a continuum. Rose, your mother, had already signs as being a great fighter herself and did not want to married or to be tied down, so she agreed to breed with the Don. She had been in love with him since they were children anyway. She agreed as long as she could leave and find her own life after. Your father by that time had already been married to that Luccus women and had that whelp. In his wisdom he could see that his legal heir would not be up for the challenges he had before him, so the arrangement was made. Rose would try to have a male child that the Don would then have to train. If you had it in you, to put you in a position to do what was going to be needed to be done. It looks like the plan has worked and produced that man. Come with me and I'll introduce you to the some of your relatives."

The next three days were some of Masso's most challenging in more ways than one. He met over a hundred direct relatives, and many people who were just members of the tribe.

"This Masso, is your grandmother, Penelope." Before him was a very old straight- backed woman with a face full of wrinkles, and just one tooth in her mouth. The one thing she did have and all the women had in common, was the two colored eyes, green with an inside ring of gold, just like the girl down at the inn.

"Come here boy, closer, so these old eyes can really see you." Her grips on his shoulders were like two pliers, "Look Jaco, he has my brother's ears," her laughter came from deep inside her. "How hung are you," she smirked as she asked? "You know my brother was like a horse, all the women wanted to try him out." The deep laughter came out once again but this time it just kept going.

"That's not any of your concern old women. We don't want to run him off this soon do we?"

At the community meal that night, Masso was asked many questions by his relatives.

"Masso, what weapons do you feel you do well with?" was asked by one of the village's trainer.

"My favorite is the staff, but the slingshot was my first weapon, and I have had a lot of success with a small blade."

"Good," replied the trainer, "tomorrow you can give the lessons on the staff and small blade, but I would personally like to see that sling shot in action."

Masso came to the training field early to warm up and gather stones for the ancient leather weapon. It was not long before the whooshing sound first, then the cracking as the stone hits its target were being heard bouncing off the canyon walls.

"You are very accurate with that, I am impressed," said the trainer. "But then those targets are not moving at you. Flouse," he yelled. An out of the corner of Masso's eye a mass began to run full speed with arms open and growling , heading right at him.

 The stone was in it leather strap, and being whipped around and around before the man had made his second step, the snap sound was heard by Masso and the trainer. The right knee received the full brunt of that stone. The large man dropped to the hard ground, rolling several times, but he jumped back up and began his pursuit again, this time with a noticeable limp and pain on his face as he took each of - the next steps. Still with forceful momentum he came. The man's third step found his left knee, knocked out from under him. Behind him another man began his assault, only to be hit in the Adams apple on his throat. The first man now back up wobbling on his two legs but still moving forward. The fist- size stone that the sling shot hurled, hit him hard and deep in his solar- plexus knocking the air out of his lungs leaving him fighting for breath.

"Excellent," the trainer said. "Men what you have witnessed is a man with three pieces of leather and a stone putting down two men, who could not get close enough to fight their battle. Let's see how use your staff now Masso." The lessons it seemed to Masso were more like a test of how good he was with these weapons than teaching a lesson.

The staff he chose was not the biggest around or the one which had the fastest action, but the oldest one with many dents from use. Swish, swish, and he is ready. The first man was smaller than he was, so Masso knew he would be harder to hit and he would be very fast. He kept his focused on his opponent eyes, for they will never lie. He took the defensive position letting the man wear himself out and to give the staff swinger time to pull out his best stuff. When the opening came he used one of his signature moves and slapped the staff hard behind both knees, and as they folded he used his staff against his back for leverage and with his own legs lifting up brought the man off the ground, shooting the body upward, before gravity took hold and slammed him hard on the ground. By the time he looked up Masso's staff was an inch from his nose.

"That move with your staff against your back, I have never seen it before," the trainer came up wanting to see it again but in slow motion.

"It is one of my own, I have several, that I have worked out for different types of situations., Like this, for enemies who are too big for me to get close enough, see that, it makes them drop their right shoulder, giving me the chance to do this. Or if I am confronted by two or three, opponents at one time I can do that. He threw the staff like a spear, and followed the staff to its destination, grabbing it back as it bounced off the targeted spot. Then with a half swing like this, I swing into the back of the next man's neck as he misses me and passes by. The last man usually is on notice, and will be careful so a simple, pass over his head and twist of my wrist will allow me to do this." Masso throws his free hand into the eyes of the man whose attention is - now on the staff, see."

"Bravo that was indeed a lesson I want to see again. You have been given good schooling and have practiced many an hour, but have you ever used them in real life situations against real men?"

"Yes, my first test was at ten years old, and I spent three years with the Sardinian Army in the last war with Austria. I fear no man and my men have been trained like wise."

As the two days of training class were given, Masso would find some of their training techniques useful as well and would be implementing them into the Alliances new training program.

Jaco came looking for him, "Masso I have come to say goodbye and to tell you that the clan has approved the lending, of four men to work as you see fit. You are a credit to your Don and our families. Keep your eyes open for the new recruits in a week or two."

The trip back through the tunnel took less than an hour this time and Masso noticed sets of wires that he did not see along the wall, before. He made one more stop before heading home. He could not leave without stopping at the Inn and get one more view of the young girl who had gotten his order.

"Your back, I see," she teased, "you must have loved our food or was it the boiling water?"

"It was the views actually. Where I come from there is nothing like them," he replied.

"Well if you see something you like you should always remember, it is here to view again, any time you want."

"I will, such beauty certainly is worth more than one viewing. I am sure I will be back, soon." Were the parting words that day by Masso , who could not figure out even why he said them to her in the first place.

The trip home was one full of deep thoughts and it was only after the rains began to really pore down did it occur to h but he changed directions and drove toward it. Masso tied up his horse under a large tree and slipped under the eaves of the building and shook as much of the excess water as possible off before going inside. The room was empty, but for the inn keeper. The large fireplace was burning hot and was the first stop for Masso. Two benches lined each side of the large open fire place Masso took the seat to the left." Inn Keeper, do you have anything to eat for a wet and cold traveler?"

"I have some leftover stew from last night I could heat up for you sir," the man replied.

"Thanks and please bring me a kettle of hot water as well." Masso yelled back as he began shedding his wet clothes, and arranging them over the bench on the other side of him to dry.

 The kettle had just been placed on the fire when the front door abruptly flew open. Two men came in and hurriedly shut the door, "Kylie bring me a brandy to warm my old body up." The older man barked out as he moved toward Masso and the fire.

The other man was already in front of the hearth, and began throwing the drying clothes on to the floor.

"I'll get those, if you don't mind not throwing my clothes on the floor," the near naked Masso asked.

"Take your wet shit and sit in that corner away from the fire. We don't need you hogging all the heat, Move on kid," and he attempted to grab Masso. Instead what he found in his open hand was a very sharp blade slicing his palm wide open, and then stuck under the man's chin very close to his throat.

"You sir have no manners and unless you wish to die here and now, I suggest you take your foul mouth and back off. There is plenty of room for us all."

"Back off, Marice" the other older man ordered. "It seems you have stuck your hand in a badgers den. Kylie, bring a clean rag for his hand and a Brandy for our young friend here."

The old man sat down across from Masso. He took a deep drink then another before he spoke. "My man's sometimes a bit too protective of me, I apologize. Marice is not used to getting push back, I am afraid."

Masso just nodded, and was not in any mood for conversation, "Thank you for the drink, sir." He just sipped the drink and enjoyed the heat the fireplace was putting out. Not having anything else to say.

"You're not from around here, are you?" The old man finally asked. The silence in the room became uncomfortable, while he waited for an answer.

"No sir, I am just passing though." was his short answer.

"Because I know most of the talent here and you would have been someone I would have known." The old man trying to engage the stranger.

"I am sure you are right, but as I said, I'm just passing through."

"To where, if I might ask?" The old man seemed to want to engage Masso.

"Piazza Armerina is where my business interest is centered, but I live on the estate of Del-La Rosa, do you know it?"

"I have not been there but her Don Leo La Barba, I had met years ago. He wanted to talk to me about a co-op type organization he was forming around the lemon business, if I remember correctly."

"Yes that is my patron, and the Alliance is a growing concern now. Are you in the agriculturel growers many services as well as security services of large estates. Have you heard of us?"

The old man continued to look at this near naked young man in front of him, noting his scared face. "My name is Don Philepo Delagleo and yes I am in the agriculture business,- cows, horses, olives, grapes, almonds and citrus, especially lemons. When you turn off the main road you find the beginning of my property and if you continue down this road in front for five more miles you still are on my property on each side of the road. "

"Masso , to my friends," the young man extended his hand. The old man took it and noted it as ruff and his own, and his hand shake firm.

"I have been hearing rumors about a gang of hoodlums moving in and forcing estates to join up for services they don't want." The old Don cautiously throws out there.

"I assure you sir, we don't force any one to join us. True there had been some conflict between a few of the estates who tried to run us off and steal our business. But those issues have been resolved in our favor. We have many small and medium orchards that have signed up and are enjoying more profit from the same amount of work. We contract the sales of our crops directly to end buyers not brokers so it is a win for all of them. We also are offering financing for our members to expand their farms. I too have heard of these gangs that seem to be out terrorizing their estates and forcing sales of produce at prices they set, but with time we hope to run them out of business. My men are men who have faced much more dangerous enemies' than a few drunken farm boys who think themselves unbeatable. We can assure our members they get honest weights, and no one is going to steal one piece of fruit from them without having to answer for it in the most severs of ways."

"Yes, Marice here can testify to that. What kind of prices did you get for your last year's lemon harvest?"

The next few hours the men ate a freshly cooked meal, shared drink and information.

"Check us out Don Delagleo, you have the name of our bank, and of several of our members. If you like what you see, contact me at the Black Rose. Together we can put in motion controlling the entire market and all of her players, think about that. You are a big player now in this small corner of Sicily, but through the Alliance, we all can be giant players in the world market, consider that.

The rest of the trip was just another normal wheel-turning journey, until Masso encountered a very handsome mule with polished hooves, standing all alone, in the middle of the road. Masso senses tuned up, *what's this fine animal doing here? Is this set up for a robbery, or maybe a scam of some sorts*? He rode the wagon slowly by, not stopping but looking around to view if he could see anyone. The mule did have a halter, and there was still a bit of rope hanging from it. Still wary he pulled the cart over and walked over to the animal. "Well young fellow where do you belong? Someone is going to miss you soon." Masso reached into his coat pocket and brought out a small green apple, "are you hungry? Yes it seems so?" Slowly, he put his hands on the animal stroking him, and talking calmly. Masso finally grabbed the short piece of rope, "Come with me Mr. Mule, and let's see if we can find your home." Using a spare piece of leather he added the two pieces together and attached the mule behind his wagon. He was only a few miles from four corners, so he headed that way.

The sight he came upon as he approached the four roads merge point was quite a view. A fancy dressed man in a green shiny silk suit was being surrounded by four young men, all over the ground his belongings were scattered. *What's going on here* Masso asked himself?' So he pulled over and jumped down, but not with- out grabbing his staff.

"Get back up on your wagon Paisa this is none of your concern." The biggest of the men shouted as he headed toward Masso waving his hands to shoot him off.

"I don't know you, and you are not my Paisa. Why does it take four of you, to go against just one pretty bird?" Masso attention went from the approaching figure to the green suited man who he now noted had a cane in his left hand. One of the men tried to grab the fancy dresser from behind, only to find the pointed end of that cane jabbing the man's gut, being pushed hard with both of the pretty man's hands. As the canes momentum stopped, the man in green's right hand slid to the top of the cane and from its interior, he pulled out a blade. With just a flip of his wrist, the steel found its home just under the chin of the man in front of him.

The big man was nearly on Masso, who swung his own wood piece against the side of his enemy's head, slapping it sideways and making the man's whole body to spin and fall.

"Thank you for your help," Mister Fancy Pants yelled out, "But I have got it from here."

He did have the leader in a position to die or back up. Masso slowly walked up to the young man as the thin diamond shape blade being stuck high on his throat. Masso leaned over and whispered in his ear, as the soon to be skewered man was trying to think how to get out of this predicament. "Are you willing to die today for your cause?"

"No" he replied, "We were just having some fun."

"Well, I guess you don't know who you decided to rob today, do you? This is Sir Poppy Cock, and you are lucky I came around to save you, from this very famous sword man, don't you think." The man said nothing. "I asked you a question; do you not understand basic Sicilian?"

"No, I mean yes, but…" the leader, now almost crying said.

"I think you all owe Sir Poppy Cock an apology, so before he allows you to leave alive I suggest you do so, don't you agree?"

The man was shaking by now and just nodded his head, "I… I am sooorry Sir Poppy Cock," he looked at the man behind him and the same words were said. The other two were in no condition to speak.

"Is that suitable Sir Cock?" Masso asked?

The man , stares hard at his opponent, steps back and makes a few fancy slashing movements with the blade, and puts his weapon back in it' s scabbard.

"Take your wounded friends and leave, but next time you try to rob or steal from someone, make sure whatever you're after is of great enough value, you would be willing to die for it." Were Masso's parting words to the four.

"Thank you sir, but I was not in any real danger, at least not from those amateurs. My name is Laurence Salvo by the way." He extends his hand out.

"Masso Del la Rosa, but if I may ask, what are you doing out here dressed like your heading to a fancy costume ball. You were just asking for trouble."

Poppy begin picking up his scattered clothes from the ground, when he noticed the mule. "Oh my you found, My Wife, "and he ran over to the mule and gave her a big hug and kiss.

"Your wife, really?" Masso is now thinking not again, *what kind of man is this one?*

"Well of course she is not my wife, but that's what I call her and she seems to like it, so you found her. She must have run off when those *Guyonos* were unloading her. She can be, a wild child, if you know what I mean?"

"I have no idea what you are talking about Poppy, but throw your stuff in the back of the cart and I think if you plan to stay around for very long, you need to get you some normal clothes. It seems from what I see here, most of your wear is not going to work here." Masso helped his new friend to brush off the dirt and put his colorful wardrobe back in leather cases, and then loaded them on the back of the cart. The trip to *Piazza Armerina* was too short a trip for this long story.

"So Mr. Salvo, what brings you to this part of the world, it must be some story."Maso asked for the curiosity was killing him.

"Well," he began, "I had a little trouble back in Palermo. My business suddenly dropped off. Then there were those two husbands, who were looking for me, and one of my boyfriend's wives. I also had a couple of personal notes coming due. So it seemed a good time to go on a vacation. My good friend Lady Campezzy had been after me to come and visit her at her country estate, so here I am..La La..."

"So where is this Lady's estate? I don't remember any family with that name around here."

"She said it was near some mountain but I forgot which, so how many could there be any way?"

"The whole island is made up of mountain after mountain Poppy Boy. Well, first let's see if we can get you some new clothes more native, so you won't stand out so much. Then I will see what we can do to locate the Campezzy family estate."

Masso parked behind the Black Rose, "You see that old green building over there. It is the dry goods store, meet me back here after you're through, and Poppy if you happen to be short of silver tell them to put it on the Big Money's account. Lastly Poppy, don't go crazy, simple is better."

Two hours had passed and still no Poppy, so Masso went to look for him. "What in the hell is keeping him, pants, shirt, belt, shoes. A half an hour and he should have been back." What Masso ran into coming out of small bar/gaming house was Poppy in his new clothes, followed by what appeared to be a young pregnant girl.

"Do I really want to know what this is about Poppy?"

"It is not like you think Masso, I won her in this dice game call" they both said "Cee- Lo" at the same time. "Yes you know it? Well I could not just let her father continued to use her as his personal cash cow, and…"

"And you gambled and won her, "Masso finished his sentence.

"Yeah," he replied, with a big smile on his face.

"So now you are responsible for her, you realize that don't you?"

"Well I really did not think that far ahead, but isn't she lovely? A beauty flower, just waiting to bloom and I do love beauty, you know." Poppy seems to drift off to dream land.

"No, I did not know of your obsession with beauty, but it should not surprise me a man who shines his, "My Wife's'," hooves. What's your name girl?" Masso ask as an afterthought.

"My name is Barlinde, and Sir Poppy Cock here told me not to worry because he had a friend who could fix anything. I am guessing that friend is you? Can you fix this? "She points to her small swelled stomach?"

"Then what," Masso asked?" You run back to your father and work the same con on someone else?"

"Lord, Mister, whatever you want to be called, if you can help me get rid of this. I will do anything you want. I don't want any screaming kid, or to become someone's mother. Please sir, what can I do to convince you? Really, anything you want? My pa has been using me as some money machine for as long as I can remember. The last thing I want to do is go back to that pig. I know how to make you feel real good I promise. I am yours if you just can help me," her hands now resting on her beginning bulge.

"Let's all go back to the Back Rose and let me think about this. Poppy, we need to have a little chat, I always can use help, but what I don't need is more problems than I already got, do you understand that?"

He left the two at the inn and went to see Mella. What he found was his mother sexually servicing the old Don orally.

He crept back out and tried to explain in his mind what he had just seen. The statement Lucia had made months ago came running back. "You and Don La Barbra are so lucky to have some like her to love you." Obviously, he thought it was a different type of love she had with the Don. He changed his game plan and headed out toward the old house just outside of town that was better known Mamma Geno's, a working girls house, which serviced the area's single men's needs.

"The madam is asleep right now sir would you like to have someone spend some time with you I can help you, do you like them blond, or full titted, or…"

"My name is Tomasso Del la Rosa and I did not come for servicing, but if you would kindly wake the Madame of the house. I will gladly pay for her time," Masso slipped the dark skinned girl a small silver coin.

Masso still had to wait a half an hour before the booming voice of the houses madam came rolling down the stair as she regally descended. "Who in the hell does this Tomasso, think he is walking me up this early in the day?" The voice of Madame Geno's fit her physical appearance, short, stout, and not very subtle. "This better be really important Mr…" Her voice stopped dead in the middle of her rant when she saw who it was. She had never met him of course, but she sure had heard many stories of the warrior who had come to town and open the casino. A man who had taken on Don Ganza, and his gang, destroying the whole group. Then the recent story of the rescue of the Delfino girl and the taking over of the Luccus estate. This must be the Don La Barba's Bastardo. "Don Del la Rosa, what an honor to have you in our humble establishment," her now honey personality came out.

"Thank you for seeing me at such an early morning hour, but it is rather important, might we find some private place to speak?" So in just a few short sentences he explained the need for a staple the women in her business always had. "So I have need of the flushing tea."

"The tea you speak of is not cheap," she began her negotiations, "And it not something a man would know how or when to and when not to administrate to the carrying mother. How young is the poor child?" Madam Geno's mind is now working overtime.

"Ok let's just cut to the chase here," Maaso not always the most patient ask, "how much will it cost for the pregnant girl to have the treatment and you looked after her. Remember a favor now can be collected latter when it is really needed and I am loyal to my friends."

"Well I can never have too many friends who owe me a favor as important as you, so let's say."

The deal was done and later that day Miss Barlinde was delivered by coach to Madam's Geno's house of pleasure.

"POPPY, get down here," yelled Masso when he got back from Madams Geno's. The man in front of him now was dressed to look like a successful worker, in a style only he could pull off. White peasant shirt, but with a bright red bandana around his neck as a tie. His new hat had Ginny hen feathers in the hat's band. His pants fit like they had been tailor-made leaving very little to any one's imagination. His horsehair woven belt had a big silver buckle, but it was his red high top boots that set him off as a dandy. As much as he tried, he could not stop laughing. "Tell me your story for their must be some reason you are so outrageous."

"Well, first let me thank you for the loan of a little cash for my new costume, don't you really love it?"

Masso just nodded his head, "it is a loan, and you will work it off at the Molti Solds, but we can discuss that latter, go on."

"I grew up in the *Sicani* Mountains hinterlands, north of *Agrigento.* My families are sheep herders. I would spend hours every day with sheep as my only friends. Some were different than others, smarter somehow. I would have all this time, so I begin brushing my favorites every day. I can tell you sheep's hair is not easy to brush, but I developed a way to work with what I had. My girls looked beautiful, and when it came time to shearing them, my girl's wool brought a premium. When I was about twelve, my father came back home from the sale of our yearly wool shearing's. He came up with the idea and explained it like this. "Boy you need to spend more of your time brushing all the sheep not just a few." He took the money from selling my lovely girls to buy more sheep. We had a big fight and I told him, "No, I will not do it." He back handed me across the room and kept hitting me all the time yelling and threatening me. That night I packed a small bag, took a couple pairs of shears and two scissors and left. I promised myself I would find a way to support myself and make animals and people beautiful and happy."

"You did not learn how to use that cane and blade in the highlands, tending sheep. So where did you pick that skill up? By the way, would you have run that blade through that man if I had not shown up and rescued you?" Asked Masso, who was trying to measure the man.

"You did not rescue me, first off. I was in total control, and I don't pull a weapon out unless I intended to use it. Now where was I? Oh yes, when I left home my destination was to any big city, lots of people, things to do, to see. Just the opposite of where I come from. I did odd and end jobs, for several years, moving from here to there, looking for something. I was not totally green but close. It was then on the way to the big city Palermo, that I met my mentor, Raul. He was a fencing master, and a wonderful teacher of many more things that just use steel. We were the talk of the town for just a short time, novelties I guess. One morning I awoke, and my mentor/ lover was just gone no note but the, 'cane', was left. I worked again at, 'whatever,' job I could get, until I was able to get myself apprenticed to a wig shop, and that place only had the cheapest clientele in all of Palermo. Some of these ladies would come in with their dogs. It became my job to keep them entertained, so I started to wash and trim. I would do their toenails which were always too long, actually most of these dogs hardly ever walked on the ground. Any way the shops business got bigger and bigger and all of these people had dogs or a cat, maybe a rabbit. I found I had a calling to make animals beautiful. I opened my own small shop, doing just animals. I was doing horses for special livestock sales or shows. I even did a man's rooster once, and you would not believe how many single men have, yep sheep. Any way I was doing very well if I can brag about myself. I began to expand and do home visits which I could charge much more. I hired an assistant to help. The home visits became much of my business and I found that some, ok, many of my lady clients wanted extra services. I was doing their animal's hair, the lady's hair and servicing many married but neglected and very sexually hungry women. Then of course a few widowed ladies."

"Lady Campezzy, being one of them?" asks Masson flippantly.

"Well no, if you must know. Anyway I started living a little too big. Then my assistant took off with all my cash. So I had to borrow from some dubious men, making payments weekly. I was wearing myself out and then two men who claimed to be husbands of some of my better customers came by the shop looking for me. I faked it and told them I was just a helper and flittered around. They never figured it out. I told them I would let, 'Me,' know. They wanted to know what services, 'I,' was providing for the bills they had in their hands. So here I am."

"You should know by now that when you take control of your own fate you are also responsible for own failures as well. So for now, your all mine, we will need to expand your skills. We have a new casino here in town and I think you will fit in there quite well. Just note, we do not take humans to cover any bets, is that clear?" Masso turned his back and motioned for him to follow.

Normally the tight group of men was not overly warm to new personnel brought into their inner circle, but Roberto seemed an easy addition, he as always around the Black Rose. Then when Masso brought in Laurence, or now and forever known as Sir Poppy Cock, or just Poppy, he just seemed to fit in as well. He was a born entertainer and with an endless supply of funny stores and with the fact he was impossible not to like. He even charmed Rizzo, the groups' natural skeptic, but in this case was glad to have him around and found he was a perfect fit for the work at the casino.

The next few months flew by. First was Divain's wedding, which was a very nice, and as classy a wedding that the area could provide. Divan's mother and father attended, the senior was greatly impressed with the estate, and kept asking lots of questions.
"Son I knew the Army would make a man out of you and now all of this without lifting a hand," The more his father kept on the madder he made Divain. After the wedding and the bride and groom left, Masso cornered the old man and sat him down. You know sir your son was part of a well-trained small force who were instrumental in winning the war. Divain's skills and courage is something you should be proud of. Your son is a real hero."

"Oh my", came a voice behind Masso's back, "My boy was actually in battles, where people were shooting, dying, really? You told me he was a cook or something safe."

 "Mother, I had no idea." The old man, tried to act innocent.

"You said he was too ashamed to come home and face us. You said he was a big disappointment to you. Well my boy a hero, did you hear what Masso said? Our son is a hero, and now a successful estate owner." She turned to face Masso now. With a

wink, whispered, "He has always been my favorite, you know."
The only happier woman that day was Grazia, but Divain's mother
came in a close second.

"Yes he was a cook, but he joined my special force and excelled.
You would be amazed at what he and that 33inch canon could,
yea well, he was in battles and performed as trained."

As Masso left the two he could hear his mother begin to rail and
unwind on Divan's father.

The day before the wedding, Masso and Poppy visited Madame
Geno's house to check up on young Barlinde. "She came through
the treatment, and all is well if that is what you're asking," The old
Madame answered when the two men called. She was a bit
surprised by their visit at all. "She seems comfortable with the
houses life and."

"And you want to keep her to work for you, is what you're
saying?" Masso asked. "She owes me, and I want to know what
she wants."

"If you want I could pay you for her debit, if it is not too much."
The negotiations began.

"First we need to speak to Barlindo, then depending what she
wants, we will see."

Masso was firm enough the Madam realized this was not an augment she wanted. *But I sure don't want to lose this girl either*, Geno thought to herself. I'll let her know you two gentlemen are here to see her. I am sure she will be glad to see you both."

In a short time a beautiful woman walked down the steps, not the little girl they left a week or so ago. She was now dressed in a beautiful ball gown and with her raised heeled shoes see seemed to float across the floor. She tried to look sophisticated, for just a brief second, but could not hold herself back. She stated giggling and the young girl in her came bubbling through. "You two should have seen the looks on your faces, when I walked down here. Don't I look all grown up? What do you think?"

"Well darling, if you let me do your hair and just a tip of color on your face I could take you into any salon or restaurant in Palermo and wow them for sure," Poppy confessed.

"More importantly what do you think, is this where you want to stay?" Masso asked in a much more serious tone.

"I know I promised you both, that if you could help me with my problem I was yours to do with as you wanted. I was desperate though, but, I will honor my word. The girls here have been wonderful, they gave me lots of their old stuff that no longer fits or things they don't want. Miss Geno is like no other woman I have known," she dropped her voice, and then whispered. "She is very smart and has promised me to teach me the whole business, she thinks I am smart enough to be her assistant and run this place."

"Barlinde, you don't have to choose this line of work. You are a smart person and could find different work", Masso pointed out to her.

"I know, but the truth is, I have been in this business for a long time. I'm not alone; a few of the other girls were used like me, and so we have a lot in common. Besides, I can take my assets anywhere I want and have something to sell that you dogs want to buy," she laughs a hearty laugh.

"Well gentlemen, what will it be, cash or trade?" The old women had been working on the girl for her entire stay, and felt she had made a good argument for her side. Knowing now, she had won.

Barlinde and Poppy went off to do her hair, and color, while leaving the two bosses to work out the details.

"Madame Geno, cash is not what I want from you or services, but what I need is information." A plan that Masso had been thinking about now he began to reveal. "Your clientele's have all kinds of information that could be useful to me. Men in drunken states and men in the throes of lust are blabber mouths. They reveal all kind of secrets, you know what I mean?" Masso watched the old woman's mind working right in front of him.

"Yes, I think I understand. Men came be very braggadocios and I have heard many things that could be of value to someone like you." *What kind of man is this he, not interested in my ladies but the left over bits of information the other men leave*? Geno now began to view him in a totally different light. *This was a real thinking man someone who is already. Oh yes getting powerful but wants more. I can see this will be a good connection for me and my girls and maybe another way to earn money selling what I get for nothing that was a lucky day for my house when that girl came in to our lives*. What do you need form me?" she replied with a smile.

"You get the information, anything that seems important and even those things that are not. I will pay you a monthly fee for this and for items that turn out more valuable I will give you bonus pay. I also bet you have contacts with other Madams in other cities. I want you to work up a network of Madams who will also share information on their clients as well. I want you to build up this network with as many houses as possible. This could be good for all of you in more ways than one, don't you think?"

The details were worked out, and with one more stipulation that Barlinde owed her nothing, and could leave any time she wanted. "One last thing Madame this information is not to be sold or passed to anyone but me. If I find out I did not get the right information, or it had been shared with others too, then I will burn that place to the ground with the madam in it."

With the girl no longer his responsibility and Divan's wedding past, Masso began making more and longer trips out across the island. He found mixed results. Most of the smaller orchards were open to joining, many just to get a chance at the Alliances bank for loans to expand or upgrade. The large estate owners that he met with, many already had hired security from local talent, or they could not yet see the need to be a part of a co-op. To some it was not much different from the organization Don Leonardo had talked about five years before. Though out of respect for Don La Barba did agree to meet or because they were curious. Several agreed to meet in order to view the man who was becoming a legend. His reputation in dealing with conflicts successfully was also widely known by now and they did not want to show Masso and his Alliance any disrespect.

The one exception was a vast estate that seemed to cover the whole north west of Palermo. All around the town of Sampogna . The families name was, Gamborino and they had their hands into everything that moved in and out of the entire area.

"What is this boy doing here?" asked the Don to his son. "I told you, I have no uses for Bastardo's trying to steal the birth rights. I own this market and nothing that group of thugs of his can help me or hurt me. They may be able to scare off a few old weak men, but we will put those dogs of his down faster than a weasel going through a hen's house. Get this piece of filth out of here. This year the market will be all mine." The Don, whose back was to Masso the whole time, was giving the rant to his own heir apparent.

Masso said nothing but turned and left, but just before the office door closed, he heard the son say, "That, father, was a stupid move on your part, he" the door closed off the rest of his words.

One more stop Masso said to himself, and as is her old house came into view, he knew he was at the right place. Bright color women's under garments hanging on the line were flapping in the wind as they dried in the sun. "Is the Madame of the house in?" This time, his arrival would be no inconvenience, for Miss K, was just finishing her meal.

"My, what a handsome young man. I bet it is your birthday and you wanted to share a little time with a real woman. Will it be your first time? It is OK Miss K will take good care of you." When she looked back into his eyes, she knew he was not here to get his cock serviced. This serious young man was probably sent by the Gamborino's to collect the rent.

"No thank you Miss K, it is not my birthday, nor do I need your services, but if I might have a short word in private?" She took him back to her small office under the staircase. She reached into a boot in the corner and began counting out dollars. "Miss K I did not come for your money either, please just relax and let me introduce myself. My name is Tomasso Del La Rose, and."

"I know who you are now, I knew you looked so familiar when I first saw you, but much younger. Your father use to come by sometimes after he had taken that old son of a bitch Don Gamborino in card games. Then he would spend some of his winnings with us. I also got a letter from Geno's last month as well. She said she needed information and would pay for it. I take it the information is for you?"

"Yes Miss K, information on any and everything you get in your sphere of influences. Especially, the Gamborino family's business, in particular, the lemon part of their operation. I need every and anything you can get." The next half an hour Masso explained what he most needed and what he could provide in the way of remuneration.

"I have hated that mean spirited evil man ever since he stole his older brother's inheritance. I would gladly do anything you need, and my girls are experts at whoring. My ladies can squeeze tubes for information and the man does not even known what he is saying. Leave it up to me you'll have all the information you ever need."

Since Masso was so close to Palermo he decided to visit Arturo La Bara the third and see if he was having any luck in putting a match for his cousin Francis." Masso, what are you doing here? Come in, come in. What brings you here to the city? Is something wrong?" Art had gotten heavier since the last time they had met so many months ago, living all that good life had given him a pudgier look.

"Well no, all is good, but I was not far from here at Sampogna, and thought I would come by to see you and find out how your search for your cousin's bride is coming along."

"You went to see Don Gamborino? I bet that did not go well, he hates Leonardo. Did you know It was him who Don Leonardo won your now famous sulfur mine from so many years ago. You showing up at his door and with that mine exploding and self-filling," Art begun howling and laughing. "I wish I had had a glass to that door. So how did that go?"

"As well as could be expected, but he revealed something I'm sure he did not mean to or even realized it. He is going to try to control the wholes year's market. He will take as many contracts for the sale of this comings year's lemons as they possibly can. Then have in their position both the contracts for sale and the actual fruit to fill the orders at the same time. They are gambling on being able to control maybe sixty percent of the whole islands production may be more. It is a gutsy move and will put the family in position for years to come to just do it again and again."

"You are not thinking of going to war against the Gamborinos are you? We are not nearly big enough to take them on now; it would be suicide, Masso."

"This coming from an army captain, think Art. You know wars are not won on one battlefield, but in many little skirmishes. It was what we did, is it not? We don't need to go to war with them, we just have to control enough tonnage by the delivery date to prevent them from delivering their contracts in full. Their penalties for non-completion will skink them. All we need to do between now and then is to buy lemons, lots and lots of lemons. When they can't deliver to the British and French fleets we will. I bet we can, getting even above top dollar, because we will have the lemons they must have. Get a message to your father to buy, buy buy. I will get with both the Alceu and Goldin banks and let them know we may need a stretch on funds this year. Let's go eat and you can tell me all about you luck finding Francis a wife."

"Dam, Masso do you ever stop thinking? Francis is no lemon that everyone wants or needs. Though, there are a few families that do have a- need of a husband for their daughters out here." They discussed each family, their, pros and cons, throughout the meal. "So I don't know, what are your thoughts?" Arturo asked in the end.

"What about the Narcisi girl, the one Rizzo rescued? Her father owes us. That match could be a good fit. Maybe he would take Francis and teach him the shipping business. Besides, it could not hurt having that connection for our own businesses."

 "Rizzo, how are we coming with the training of the new men?" yelled Masso as he came through the doors of The Big Money late that afternoon.

Masso looks ruff and tired, thought Rizzo at first. Rizzo hoped this last campaign out, was a success. He felt it must have been, because Masso sure was not argumentative. "Yeah Boss they are doing great now that your Tin Men are here and running the school."

"Great, because we are going to need a lot more after this last trip? Also I want to get with Art and the Goldin's and set up a couple new trading companies to do nothing but to buy this year's lemon crops. Use different names so it will not seem we are trying to steal the market, but we are. The Alliance now has an additional goal buy every single lemon we can, on this island."

 He put Charlie, Gerome, and even Rizzo, out on the road during the weekdays hunting for members and looking to buy lemons. Divain, despite being busy learning as much as fast as he could about the agriculture business, he made it a point to reach out to the neighbors introduce himself and pitch the Alliance. Masso too was busy traveling and closing memberships and pushing the team. The more people heard the pitch and had heard of the success the Alliance was making, the easier it was to get new members. Which meant more men, which means more training, which all will equal more power in the end and bring Masso one step closer to achieving his mission for his Parton.

A month after Masso visit to Sampogna and Don Gamborino things began heating up. Masso walked into Black Rose that night and in his office he found mail.   One from Palermo, that Arturo had written. Another letter from Catania, this one from Gabbriel Alceu, the last letter was from Don Arturo La Barba. Eyes wearied, body screaming for rest and *yet a few more things to do before I sleep tonight*, he thought to himself.

The first letter open was from Don Arturo,

Dear Masso, Just a short update on the progress of the trading side of the families business. The office was back open in Palermo, under the Old trading company's original name, "La Bara Trading Company." The operation is being run by Alberto. Arturo is now coming in to help and learn the business now that the Don is back at De la Rosa. Antonio tells me the new sales offices and the warehouse at the dock in Catania is near completion. What you're not going to like to hear thought, is, the project is costing way over our budgeted amount. Alceu has approved the additional moneys to complete the project. At least we will be ready to receive and ship our lemons at harvest time. The warehouse at the docks in Scilla is still operation. She is still making a little money, so I am spending my days there. Sales of our sulfur have been tepid, due to slow demand, but there are rumors the market will turn around any time now. Please send me as soon as you can the anticipated numbers of tonnage of citrus we can expect to be coming in. On another note, I have not been getting a good response from Hector or Felix Goldin. I made payment s on two of our outstanding loans, but even so, nothing. Not like them, I usually get some kind of acknowledgement from one, Zero? I'll get back to you on that as soon as I can go by the bank and see what is what. Lastly, I have had a few inquiries because of Francis. They wanted to know if Arturo had the authority to negotiate on his marital availability. I have replied to each that the families Abortrador, has given Arturo the job of finding a good marriage for Francis La Barba.

Will let you know more as soon as I have some more information.

Sincerely

Don Arturo La Barba

He picked up Arturo's letter and he read the short note.

Masso, I have had a few serious inquiries regarding potential marriages for Francis. A reoccurring problem though, seems to recently be coming up. Wild stories are going around, lots of rumors, all of a sudden. Stories of private armies rooming the rural lands forcing pay- offs for protection. Kidnappings for ransoms of young girls and of their mutilations. Old women being forced to do unthinkable acts. Large cannons blowing up rescue parties. Unfortunately, the stories go that the famous Bastardo Warrior, of the family, is leading the charge for the La Barba family that is it. I have tried to explain but roomers grown their own feet, as you know.

The suggestion of Don Narcis though, is possibly a good one. I have plans for lunch one day next week to meet with him at his club. I guess his daughter is becoming a bit of a handful. She also does nothing but talks of the Del La Rose family's estate. I will get back to you on that.

Always Arturo

The third letter did not bring any good news.

Tommasso Del La Rosa,

Sir, it is my duty to inform you that the Alceu family's financial branch is with- drawing support from the, Alceu Alliance Bank.

 Please arrange payments for any outstanding amounts due.

Yours Truly,

Gabbriel Alceu

Vice President

This was not good news to go to sleep by he said to himself, "Tomorrow."

"There is something going on, I can feel it," Masso was addressing the group at the next morning's breakfast. "Poppy go and see Madam Geno, bring me back the gossip, on the lines? Charlie go by and see Lucia, see what she might know. Gerome ride to the Goldin's bank and get to the bottom of their issues. Rizzo put whatever men you can in the three key area s we planned. Send one Tinman to each regiment, to help and oversee our three biggest territories. Roberto you need to take over the Big Money, while Rizzo is away. Rizzo, I need you to run a special mission." All right meet back here soon." Rizzo", Masso pulls him away from the others. "I need you to go to Palermo, and reach out quietly to Miss, Narcis. Someone is intentionally spreading lies about the Alliance and us. They are distorting the truth, and spreading outright falsehoods. See if you can find the source, she probably would have a good idea. Then deal with it so it is no longer a problem."

"Sure Masso." *In his mind though he is thinking, I have not seen her in so long, but I can't get her out of my mind and I will be looking forward for this assignment.*

Masso sent each of the two Arturo's a quick note with explicated instructions for each of them. He then left for Catania, to address the banking issue himself. He got to town just after the bank closed down. His first stop was to the home of Don Carmine, "The Don and his wife are out of town," the old women who answered the door, replied.

"Do you know where they went and when they are due back" asked Masso?

"To Spain to visit the Misses family, I believe for just a couple of months, she was beginning to wish he never answered the door tonight, *this man is scary*, she thinks.

"If I might ask for that address to send him a gift, and I'll be on my way."

"I sorry sir but, I don't think,"

Masso looked directly into her eyes and then pushed his way in. "You will get me that address or," Masso had pumped himself up giving the appearance he was much larger than he actually was, "NOW women, now."

The first stop that next morning just as it opened, was the bank.

"I'm sorry sir, but the Don is not available and young Gabriele, probably will not be in at all today. Is there something I might do for your sir?"

"Why yes, please give him this box, a gift of sorts, ask him to contact me, so we can finalize this year's business that his father and I contracted about. " Masso left heading towards the family's newest acquisition.

 "Antonio, this looks great, you have the old shoe plant looking like a traders paradise. The docks I see were repaired and now we just need lots of lemons to fill all this empty space. My job I guess."

Late that day, the younger Alceu, slipped into the back way of the Bank. *You can never be too careful*, he thinks to himself. He goes to his office only to find a plan card board box on his desk, "What have we here, something from mom already?" He opened the box to find a single well-made, new Tin Cup. What the hell is this?" As he lifted the dull cup out of the box a simple white business card falls out. The Bastardo, father was right a letter was not going to work, and now it is up to me to weigh the choices. Do we go all in with banking cartel and break our word and written contract? Then know that our lives will be in danger forever, that cup made that clear, that is no idle threat. Or give them just enough to hang themselves, but not succeed, like father suggested? Whose wraith can we survive? I will have to post a letter tonight and advise dad.

He planned to spend the night at the estate and have, "THE" talk with Mella, he had been putting off for the past few months. The accidental sighting of her and his Don engaging in sexual activity still left him more questions than answers. Over dinner they talked of the progress she had brought to the orchards and how the improvements to the main house were finished. As the conversation quieted down, Masso brought up the issue. "Mella, I came by a few weeks ago and found you and the Don in an intimate position. I left but it has bothered me ever since."

"Intimate position; are you too shy to say I was sucking his cock? I am a woman too, besides being your mom. You have gotten half of your story, from your new family, but there is our side. I grew up on this land, following my mother around like you use to follow me. Learning all I could from her. Leonardo was older than me and I would watch him follow Augusta like you did too. I knew he and I were from two different worlds, but I had my little girl fantasies. I fell in love with him. We would spend time together occasionally; he would tell me about the books he was reading or of the things he had done that day with Augusta. We became friends. Leonardo would ask my opinion on different things and seemed to respect my advice, because he often would follow it. Then damn it all, if it did not turn out to be the best choice. Latter he went to Palermo to finish his studies and training for the business. When holidays came around or harvest time came around we would work side by side, picking fruit or putting up Christmas decorations. We were inseparable. Then came the black period, when Leonardo's father was going through his craziest period. It was when the old Don became so desperate that he put Leo up for sale to the highest bidder. He died before he could complete any contracts, so Augusta became the families Abortrador. He finished the job to find the best deal he could for the family. That money was put back into the orchards, enabling them to go back into full production an also allowing the estates to purchase back a few smaller parcels adjoin us. My Leo was then a married man. He would though, still come to me, to get my advice on many different things. His new wife only came here once, stayed two days and left. Francis was born soon after they were wed and within a year or two the Don knew the boy would never be up to the challenges of being a strong Don. Even as a child Francis was spoiled and whiny. He would run away from confutations and like his mother hated the rural living and its primitive existence. The Don came to me with his worries and knew he only had a few short years before Francis would be of legal age and take over everything the Don had worked so hard to build back up. So we came up with the plan, you sort of. The Don to have another child from a different but strong woman and if that child was, not a girl. Then maybe this child, a male, might be able to be molded and taught to be the strong leader the family would need for the future. Someone who could come along and clean up any messes that Francis and his brother- in -laws would be creating. I volunteered to carry his seed. We became physical lovers, with a purpose. I loved him and anyway I could be a part of his life even if it was only as a mistress and breeder. Back then I did not care. I cherished our time together, and mourned when he was not here. He and I tried for over a year. We were like rabbits, every time we could get away. We were doing it, all over this estate. That was certainly the best year of my life. Nothing happened though, so I came up with the suggestion of a Cummari's, he knew. Rose, the Tin Men's women he had known, so the deal was made. After you were conceived, the Don married me off to Augusta as a reward to him for his years of loyalty. I got you as my reward, and it has allowed me to stay close to him."

Masso just sat quietly for the longest time, trying to put the picture together. "It now makes sense, but now."

"Now is now, he is not dead, he is a man. Men have needs that need to be taken care of, even men like him. You must have seen us being tame, you should see when I..."

"Yeah mom, that's more than enough information for me, thank you very much. So I was just a piece in this man's long- term plan." *Jaco had been right*, Masso thought back, and tried to make a deeper sense of the picture emerging now with the new pieces added.

"Don't hate us son," Mella could see the wheels turning in his head. "Know you were created for a purpose, but never think you were not loved. Your Don truly fell in love, probably the first and only time he was truly and totally in love in his life. When he looked down upon you for the first time, your green and gold eyes staring back at him. I saw such a look of pride and love. I was jealous at first, but you won his heart totally and mine. You were a gift to the whole estate."

"Well at least I know the whole story. So tell me Mella, is he still in there? Can you see anything more than a body left?"

"Yes he is still there. He may not speak words but we talk every day. Sure I do all the speaking but I can tell by looking into his face and those eyes. They answer me back. You just keep what you are doing, follow the plan and, well, time will work everything out, my son."

"I do need one more thing from you. I need several gallons of Faustina Avveleniamo."

"Are you planning and killing half of this island? Why so much?" Her brain picked up, *what he is up to now?*

He began to outline the last few weeks' worth of work, the most recent events and his new defense plans. "So you see where men can't be twenty- four hours a day my little solders can and for much less cost."

"A good plan, I will start today though it may take me several days to make this much, but I will have the first batch ready by tomorrow night."

Around the table was Arturo who came with Rizzo, just back from Palermo after completing his work. - Gerome, Charlie, Divian, Roberto and Poppy, "What goes on in this room stays in this room, and what information is revealed here today can make or break us, so tell me only the truth ,not, plus anything else. Poppy what did you find out at Mamma Geno's?"

"She said almost immediately after your business with her, she sent out letters to the other madams she had connections too and they in turn reached out to others, and so on. First she told me to pass on the message, "do not totally trust Miss K. She may be milking both cows." She told me that you must have really pissed off Don Gamborino. The word is he hated you flaunting your power. You who was just a piece of dog dung Bastardo. He thinks you stole away the power from the legitimate Don Francis. He even claimed if it had been Francis who came to him to join the Alliance he would have given it serious thought, but when you came in, it made him feel sick to his soul. So it seems he has decided to destroy you and everything you and the family has in order to protect the Sicilian way. Kill it at the root before it spreads."

Gerome, what did you find out about the Goldin's?"

"Well they too were put off by your first encounter with them. The Don never needed to be so forceful, let's say. Then it seems there is a cartel of bankers, who knew? They seemed to have a lot of influence behind the scenes in the money lending business. Seems word went out that the family was toxic and for no one to do business with us or any of our extended businesses. They don't think it wise to buck the power."

"Charlie what is the word in the orchards these days, what did Lucia have to say?"

"She sends you her love first, then there something we need to know about, yeah ok, the business first. She said there have been a lot of strangers in the area and they have been spreading rumors about the Alliance and how it will not be around when the harvest comes, and they need to remember Don 's Gamborino's generous offer or else."

"I have had the same types come into our area as well," Divain said.

"There has been similar talk coming and going, questions asked at the casino lately too," Roberto blurters out.

"Rizzo how was your mission?" Masso ask at last.

"It went as you expected, though it turned out we had two different parties spreading bullshit. Francis, complaining to anyone who will buy him a drink and listen to his woes. Then the real wave maker though, was a real social butterfly. His family is tied to a very old banking group in *Palermo*. They have connections with the Gamborino family thought marriage. He was a big fixture on the social scene in *Palermo.* I heard he was found bled to death with his tongue cut out just before I left."

Arturo did you bring the first order of weapons I requested?

"Yes, we brought them back and I must say it is brilliant idea. It will reduce our need for solders."

"Good I want you and Divain to plan out where each one goes and over see their installation, take a different man there, each time you go out over the next few days. I want everyone to be familiar how to set them, and men the poison is deadly so be very careful when handling them. We are now in a war and it has already started. This one is for all the pie, so no slip ups, no letting downs."

The next few weeks were busy. Masso made trips back to visit and reassured each member of the Alliance. He personally explained the defenses that were being brought into their orchards and how it was going to protect their crop and for them to stay clear of the treated areas. He also made his appearance to both of the banker families. This time, not threatening but with an offer that had to be taken seriously. Profitable enough to risk going against the banking cartel. All along, Masso still continued to reach out to more and more small family orchards.

The first confutations came quick when five of the contracted orchards were invaded by some of Gamborino's men. They came to cut down some of the orchard's trees. Instead they got a big surprise. Man traps had been set all along the perimeter of each of the properties and the paths that were used to work the orchards. Wagons and tree stumps or large rocks strategically placed, forcing the invaders to follow the deadly trapped routs. Pits dug into the ground with steel sharpened nails protruding upward from the pit's bottoms. Each nail coated with Mella's deadly potion, each pit covered with small thin sticks and then covered with bark, leaves, and grasses, just like the rest of the ground around them, invisible to most eyes and totally undetected at night when the invaders came. The second surprise came to the majority who did not find themselves impaled. Land mines, which took out many legs and body parts when just one, went off. The Alliance's forces were not near any of the attract sites, but the next morning's body counts and opened holes where the poisoned, man traps had been set, leading Masso to calculate somewhere between thirty to fifty men were killed or would die soon between the five sites. One thing Masso knew, the seriously injured would soon wish they were dead.

The next move the Gamborino's, were reportedly going to make was full frontal attack. This was the Intel Masso got from both Miss K and from another independent source of Mamma Geno's. "We maybe undermanned, to cover all the bigger estates, but, I have another plan. Tonight we will, begin some mental war fare, scarecrows dressed as armed men will be placed around the roads leading up to some of these estates; bonfires will be set up along the backsides of these estates giving from the roads the appearances of large armies waiting for them. We may not be able to arm all of our people with rifles or pistols, but I have made up many multi firing cross bows, that are very simple to use, cock, aim, shoot, repeat."

The following night several small and five larger estates were attacked. They were met with more defensive forces than expected, and all of the invading forces were met with another ancient tactic. Large bronze highly polished shields which when fires were lite in front of them reflected bright light that could be directed into the faces of the invading trespassers, blinding them and making the men easy targets for the defenders. They too manage to capture two of Gamborino's men. The real damage came at Del La Rosa. Multiple-fires were set throughout the orchards and so all the available people were busy fighting fires leaving the house unprotected. Two assassins entered the main house to kill the old Don who they found in his library. What they did not expect to find was the old woman. Mella was also there with her Don. She without hesitation jumped in front of her lover taking the blow of the shot that one   man was able to get off before they got the taste of her Lupara. She shot both men ending both of their lives and mission. Mella died content, at her Don's feet. Satisfied she saved her Leonardo and the future of Del La Rosa.

Masso was now a man with a new vengeance, "Up until now," he told the group," We have played defense, no more."

"Masso, your tin- men have been busy with the captured men and quite successful. We have the names and locations of all of the Gambino's men, it only took three fingers and half a foot on one of the men to get him to talk, and the other when confronted by the soon loss of his pride and joy, his large cock, sang like a little girl."

With the map of the area and the locations of each member of Gamborinos, residences laid out. Masso gave his orders and assignments for his plans actions. "They started this war, now they will soon regret everything they have tried to do, to destroy us." The men were divided into teams of twos.

Divain and Gerome's assignment was the home of Don's Gamborino's number two man, his cousin the planner. Just before sunset, with the thirty- three inch cannon in position and loaded, Gerome began the raining of terror. The first shots took out the front door of the house and the second hit took out a big part of the second floor. As the targets tried to flee the now burning house, Divan would pick them off with his rifle or scare them back into the inferno. The death count here was seven; five adult men, one women and one child.

Charlie and Poppy's destination that night was Don Gamborino's own estate. The residence sat in the middle of a fifteen- acres track surrounded by a tall rock wall that defended the residence. The last month Masso knew a final battle would come. In prep he had Mella working much of that time to make pigs blood by the gallons. This ancient incinerate burned hot and for many hours, the most impressive factor was it could not be put out with water, or by throwing dirt to suffocate the flames. Poppy and Charles poured the liquid all along the inside of this tall rock barrier. When lite it put the homestead in the middle of a ragging ring of burning very hot fire. This three hundred and sixty degree visual they had to watch in sheer terror, also now wondering what was going to happen next.

The Rizzo, Masso twosome, used a large cross bow that launched speared arrows covered in Pigs blood and a Catapult mounted sideways on a wagon. The rocks it flung were also wrapped on cloth soaked in the incinerate oil. The planed staging area was on a rise in the middle of the concentration of workers homes. Now within striking distance, the two fire flinging weapons began their aerial assault. With no defense they helplessly found that in less than a half hour ten of their homes were burning and would never be inhabitable again. Those that did not die would have to face the coming winter homeless.

The three tin men were busy too making house calls to the other four members of Don Gamborino's immediate family. Two were garroted, one had his throat slashed and the last one drowned in his horse's watering trough.

The morning of the third day the group met and though successful in their work, no glee or joy was being felt by anyone but Masso.

With only a couple of weeks till the first harvest, the crunch came to both the Alliance and Gamborino. Masso had run out of cash money to pay for the last tonnage of lemons that would make sure his opponent could not reach his goal. Also now his credit was being squeezed shut by the banker's cartel's pressure.

In the middle of all the chaos Arturo came in with an offer from Don Narcis, "This may be your best and only offer you're going to get for Francis. This war we are in has all the other families who might have been interested, instead are backing off. Funny thing though, it did not defer my meeting with Don Narcis.

 In fact, he told me, "My experience with the La Barbra family has been quite surprising. You could have easily held Antonetta for ransomed, or even sold her to someone. What you did instead made sure she was protected and then made sure she made it home safe and intact. You also took care of my family's biggest problem, Braggio. The war with the Gamborino's does not worry me. I myself having been in many business battles, I know what it takes, if you're going to land on top. I personally admired your families back bone for not rolling over like most people your size would of have done against the larger organization. I think if Francis agrees it could be good for both families."

 On the other item you requested, I sent each of the Bankers in the cartel one tin cup to their offices, and one to their homes address to their wives."

"Good, we need to start re-educating those smart asses. What could he have on them or use for collateral? Damn it, he has put his property up. I am going to send a Tin Man back with you; he can accompany you while you start visiting the banking houses that are backing his gamble. Push them to understand it is not for their best financial health to continue funding Don Gamborino. Let them know he does not have the legal authority to take loans on the estate's orchards, and or any of the rest of the families' assets. Only the legal heir can do it. And the only legal heir to that estate is his older brother Phillip. If they don't have Phillip's signature, they have nothing. Then let them know, that Phillip will never agree to this move. As of right now they do not even have the harvest of his trees for collateral. Now Poppy time for you to return to Palermo quietly, except this time to meet a new friend, here is Phillip Gamborino's current location. Introduce yourself, get close to him and invite him to share some fun times. All you have to do is keep him occupied with whatever is his fancy, at least as long as you don't leave the residency or are seen. If they can't find him they cannot get his signature on anything. Though maybe he will sign some papers for us," Masso thought out loud.

Like the others, Masso too had a list of people to see.

 "Don Delagleo, thank you for giving me a moment of your time, I know you have already started harvesting your grapes, and getting ready for the big lemon harvest so I really appreciate it." Masso meets the old man at the same old inn but in much better weather.

"How is Don Leo? I heard they came into his house and tried to kill him. Is that true? We certainly are living in different times from when I got into this business. You know though, you are the reason for all upheaval. Stuck your whole hand into Gamborino's big pie, and when he tried to grab it back; you cut it off at the wrist. At least that is what I have been hearing." The old Don laughed at his own joke.

"Yes if it had not been for my mother Don Leonardo would have been dead now. Instead she gave her life for her Don." Masso took a moment before he, in a more aggressive tone, continued. "Know this, I did not gamble on trying to cornering the whole lemon market and the Alliance did not start the war. As you know I am a man who has seen battle up front and in person. There is no start n stop. Once it's started only one can win, no matter how much you hate doing what is needed to be done. War is not nice but in the end it's the ones who are left standing that are the winners and in any war all the dead are just a part of getting there. So Don what is the talk out there among your compadres?" Masso asked concerned this war may have hurt the legitimacy of the Alliance with the bigger orchards.

"Well truth be told, many are happy someone has finally taken on the Gamborino's. The family has been a threat to even us in the past and now you came along. I have heard he is close now in getting enough fruit to fill all his contracts, but you have pulled your fingers from that dike with your Alliance. Your members were the tons he counted on to put him over the top. He also was counting on picking this last tonnage for a bargain. That's where he thought he could make a killing, getting his biggest profit margins off of them. So Masso, what next?" asked Don Philepo.

"Next is to make sure he does not have any way to fill his biggest contract the one with the British Navy. If he fails he will be done. That is why I am here. To find out if any one you know will buckle and throw in with him?"

"Well, who knows what any one of us will do under the right pressure, Masso? What I can do is get you the list of the most vulnerable, but you don't want to be the threat that pushes them toward him either."

"I see your point. So we will send a reassuring message, one of support, good call. What are you going to do? Pick up a contract that is still out there now or hold off and wait and see what the market will bear?"

"My target price, you know, so I am going to wait, and hope you succeed, but as soon as it hits my selling price,then I am, all in, whether it is to you or someone else. So go get you some more money boy and come back soon." The old Don laughed again.

 Back in Palermo in the office of La Barba Trading Company, Francis found himself alone after a ten week trip around the continent. He had used his connections from the past to start putting small deals together or taking a small finder fee's instead of big pay offs or big losses, simply by putting buyers, and sellers together. It was not the big deals he was used to, but the success was more fulfilling somehow now that he did it totally on his own. With no help from his twin's uncles and without the feeling his father was looking over his shoulder, judging him for every decision he made. Most of his mail was still bills but an invitation from his cousin Arturo to meet and discuss an important family matter did perk his interest a little. *What is he up to?* Francis asked himself, *He can't have found anyone who would be so desperate to pay any amount to have a La Barba as a son in law. That crazy Bastardo has done me a favor there. Tomorrow, at eight, my office,* Francis, was the message he sent promptly back.

Upon getting Francis's reply that he was back in town, and would gladly meet him at the Palermo office at eight the next morning. *That is awfully early for Francis*, Arturo thought. *He never gets up before noon, so this is something new for him. Hum, I wondering what caused this radical change?"*

Waiting for Arturo at the office, was strong coffee and a selection of cannoli and cassotelle's cut fruit, cheese and breads. "Come in Arturo, join me before we get down to, family business, is it?" Francis warmly welcomed his older relative.

"Who are you and where is my cousin Francis, you're at the office this early and offering all this," as he pointed to the elaborate spread that was before him. "What is it, have you found Jesus or what?"

With a small laugh Francis replied. "No but I have found a way to pay my own way. So I guess I have found a way to God of sorts, the Gold God. "

Over broken bread the two share stories of their lives. Arturo told of his years in the military, of the pettiness and backstabbing among the officers and top commanders who had very little training and no real military knowledge. "The three battles I commanded had some of the best trained men you could have asked for. Fighting against frontal attack were men, who were fighting for the idea of independence for their families and country. Men that you and I know will never get what they think they deserve. These men fought on ground filled with dead and dying and screaming wounded men. Grounds soaked with blood, and shit, bile, they fought for hours against equally stupid men. Those men, who were dying for an idea, of the importance of keeping some Hun, born in the right place and time, as Emperor.

The military has taught me many things good and many realities of life."

"My lessons were less physical in nature more mental. My father never had much time for me, so my two uncles we my guides, to man hood. There is a downside to having too much. My mother's brothers, the twins never wanted for anything. The Luccus family as you know are old family rich, land, manufacturing and well, you know I am sure. So the family bought a groom for the unwed older daughter, and a trading company for the twin boys to play with. Now they could say to the world, we are successful businessmen. Two problems solved with just one purchase. After my mother passed so did the family's interest in me, no more bail outs. It made me smarter I guess the reality that only I myself could get me through this. The last six months I started over, and well I am getting by, and it feels good too. So Cousin what family business needs to be discussed?"

"Does the name Don Narcisi, mean anything to you? The families in shipping, asked Arturo, in his mischievous voice.

"I leased the estate to one a few years back, never met him, Braggio, I think was his name."

"Yes, well it is his Uncle who has a daughter who needs a husband and he has shown an interest in you."

"So the Bastardo, is going to saddle me with the Narcisi family's cur, a real dog I bet. How desperate they must be to reach down in the dirt, to find me."

"Actually, Francis she is quite lovely, you two could make beautiful children together. She is young and a bit head strong. Her father Don Louis Narcisi told me, he has no way to control her." His exact words were. "I hope her being married to a strong man and having a few brats sucking on the teats, will make her happy." She is a prized beauty though. I also know there are no males in the line to control the family's future businesses interest. I'm going to level with you. The family needs this to work. The cash it will bring in, inject of capital we need to secure the tonnage of lemons the Alliance needs to win this war. No one can force you to marry anyone, but sacrifices sometimes in our lives must be done. Just for the betterment and good of the whole family. Look your own father sacrificed and married your mother, so the La Barba family's home and business could live." Arturo was being totally honest with him.

"So my father's Bastardo, sent you to sell me on family and future. Why should I? That son of a bitch has taken over everything. He is getting rich and using that bull shit title Arbortrardor as his power source to get us in a war with one of Sicilia oldest families of Gabellotti {Middlemen} on top of it. Just to prove he is a La Barba. Sorry but it seems like there is no hope for the family to me. That Bastardo has gone against hundreds of years of tradition. He and my father are crazy thinking they can change the way things are and always have been."

"You have a couple of miss conceptions Francis. Masso has made no moneys from any of his actions. In fact, whatever monies he has made, he put back into the families businesses. He could have put the sulfur lease in his own name, but he did not, it is in the Don's. Never has he ever even clamed your father as his own, he simply calls your father his patron. I understand you anger. I do. You are the oldest, and the one who should be doing what Masso is doing. Francis, when I was talking about the men in my command. Masso and his private trained men were some of those men I spoke of. He and his group of troublemakers were personally responsible for our side winning the war. No one will tell him that, but it was true. I was there when they were destroying the enemy's lines. They opened up their whole right flank allowing our troops to pinch in the Austrians. The group then came up behind the Austrians lines stopping up the only way for them to retreat. Mella, his mother died protecting your father. Everyone has given up something special to make this whole idea of your father's, work. Masso is the only one who could have gotten this far, and he is very close to getting this done. The Don was right when he appointed him to the post. That Bastardo, he has done what no one I know of, even your father could have done. In the end, it will be you who have to make the decision. It is you who now holds all the power. You choice will determine the whole family's future just as your father had done."

No answer was given that morning but Arturo's message the power in this play has just switched to the future Don La Barba.

Back at the dining room of the Black Rose, the remaining group ate in silence, waiting for someone or something to break the ice. When Masso walked in the whole group seemed to sit up looking for good news. Rizzo was the last to join the group. "I got a message that Gamborino wants to talk and see if something can be worked out before this battle destroys both of our families."

"I don't trust that old brother fucker, so make the meet in Father Stefano's church, at noon, just he and I. Also I want," the instructions were specific, and detailed as Masso had already worked out the details almost as if he knew what was coming before even the opponents did.

At noon the Don Gamborino's only son walked in to the Chapel, Masso was already waiting in the basement apartment of the padre.

"Thank you Don Del La Rosa for this meeting my…"

"Your father did not seem fit to meet face to face with me, as was the terms. I then have to conclude he is not really serious about ending this conflict." Masso was stern and forceful without having to raise his voice.

"No sir, it is nothing like that, he was not feeling well enough to make it today. He has authorized me to make a deal. He is very anxious to bring this to an end. He is willing to pay you this much over todays current market prices for your harvest."

"He is willing to pay that price for the entire Alliance's inventory?"

"Oh no, I'm sorry if I did not make myself clear. It's only your family's estates lemon's that we would purchase at the premium. We could not afford to buy anyone else's."

"In that case," Masso quickly replied, "none of our tonnage is for sale at any price. We are going to wait and see what the market will bear after the contract's deadlines. You might as well take a copy of this document to your father as well. This one has been signed by the real Don of the Gamborino's family, Phillip Gamborino. It is a sales contract to the Alliances for all this year's harvest of lemons from your family's estate. The British Navy's office of purchasing also has copy of it. They have removed the Gamborino tonnage which you have already delivered, thank-you very much by the way, from the total tally owed on your contract." Young Gamborino now, was visibly defeated as he sat there.

"What do you want, Mr. Del La Rosa?" The young man asked. Knowing there was not going to be an answer he or his father, was going to like hearing.

"Nothing," was Masso's only reply.

In the churches bell tower was Rizzo and in a tall cypress tree across the street was, Divain. The instructions were to look out for hands signals from Gamborino, and to watch for assassins that he felt would be close by. The sun was directly overhead and made the tree and tower dark and undetectable, but would put the most light on the men who were sent to assassinate. Masso snuck out the back wearing the priest spare clothes, knowing that the men who were out there would never attack a priest.

In time, the two men sent by Gamborino got impatient. They came out of hiding and headed toward the Churches' front door with guns in hand. Both were shot dead before they knew what hit them. The third assassin, who was to cover the back door, took off running before the third shot could be made.

Back at the Gambrino's estate, late that night, "How can things get any worse? That Bastardo has scared our banks, they are pushing hard for their money back. Some have even filed liens with the British buyers. They want me to come up with real legal collateral, so no more cash to finish buying the needed tonnage even if I could find the fruit? Now he has my brother, who knows where, and got the simpleton to sign over our own tonnage. I should have held off picking till the last minute. He seems to constantly be one or two steps ahead of me at every turn. He probably would have shot me if I had been there today. Every time I think I have him cornered, he appears somewhere else and cuts us down. Who does he think he is? He is not even a legal heir to the La Barba family. The job of Arbortador has always been only for Men of Honor, Umoini Donare. Men whose families have for generations been doing this job, first for the vast Laitfundia. [Vast landowners]. Their absentee landowners could live in their mansions elsewhere and be assured their representatives were collecting the rents and handling the problems. From the beginning I knew that La Barba was going to be a problem, as it has turned out his movement has been a much bigger problem than even I had envisioned. What does he want?"

Outside the tall rock wall surrounding the same estate, Gerome and Charlie are prying open the hatch to the escape tunnel, that lead back to the house. "Masso sure has a deep Sicilians' sense of **VINNITTA,** [vendetta]. If we start the fire here on the bottom of the steps, once it gets going strong all we need to do is continue to drop wood and then the sulfur on the blaze . Where do you want me to set the cannon up for you?" Gerome asked.

"Up between those two lone trees, should give me enough space to launch the attack with the cannon, we will set her up first, then start the fire. When the fire is burning hot enough we will begin to launch the assault." Charlie was not as sure of the plan as Masso seemed to be but, he had not led them wrong once yet.

They had brought enough kindling wood with them to start a good size fire, and a small container of pigs blood to make sure it would start and burn even in this damp cavernous hole. Swish and then combustion, the fire burned hot right from the start. The boom of the cannon's blast, echoed off the walls of the surrounding the estate's home." Well they know were here now," announced Charlie. "Did you see where it hit? All I can see is smoke."

"You hit where the boss wanted. It looks as best as I can tell the right rear quarter of the roof, is totally gone. Start adding the sulphur to the fire and stand back and whatever you do, don't breathe any of that smoke."

The burning fire's smoke began to fill the cavernous trail that led back into the house. As soon as the roof was opened it created a natural pump, the hotter air filled now with smoke rising as it is sucked into the house. Then as warm air does it would rise, and then would seek an outlet like a chimney. The house's new chimney was now the large hole the cannon had just made.

Once the sulfur was added, it began producing laced gases, that when mixed with the water from moist walls of the tunnel created a poisonous gas smoke, which now was being pumped deep into every room of the family's stately home, a certain death.

Deep in a root cellar the old Don and his Goomara [mistress], hid, having made it there only because they were in the kitchen when the attack began. "I have totally underestimated this Diablo, he has destroyed everything my family has created in the last hundred years. I will kill him if it is the last thing I do, I swear on my dead families' honor, if we get through this."

News of the heinous attack was known from one side of the island to the other in a very short time. The government sent brigands to try to stop the open war fare. In days things were back to normal but it was now only three days till the British Navy's contract was due in full for Gamborino. "The Don survived, it was a good plan Masso, but you know luck cannot be accounted for in these matters. Now for more bad news, two of the old Gabellotti families that Don Delagleo had on his list that might cave just pledged their crops to him." Was the news Rizzo gave his friend.

"Backlash, I guess, like Don Delagleo, warned me about. Well if my information is right he still needs tonnage, and we need cash. I need to make a trip to Palermo and see if I can work a miracle or two," were the words Masso spoke as he headed out the door.

In the offices of La Barba trading the future Don of the family was about to leave for the day. Francis had finally made up his mind. *The final attack by my father's Bastardo has made that decision easier. I am sure the wedding deal will be off the table and our family's name will be ruined anyway.* Francis thought to himself. Just before he reached for the handle of the door, it opened. "What are you doing here? I will not be bulled even by you. We are done, so go back to whatever hole you came out of."

"I have not come to bully you but to give you a choice. All of your the families future depends on this choice. The Cheezo family has sold their mine to some British group. Your farther holds the lease, which I now control. They have made me a very fair offer for the remainder of the lease. It will more than cover the money the Alliance needs to finally prevent the Gamborino's from filling their order with the British Navy. Or…"

"Or what," Francis said, "you think Auturo can salvage the proposal of Marriage, you must be crazy as well as being a heartless killer."

"You have been mad at your father because he gave me so much of his time,time you felt was yours. You have always taken it out on me, fine. You may not have had his time, but you had his love. Why do you think he set things up the way they were? I was just a prize breed animal, trained like a sheep dog to perform. From the time I was crawling I was being primed for the job, a job you or anyone in this family could not do. I was killing men at age ten and in the army at age thirteen. I was taught critical thinking, not to make me a better person, but to be able to calculate aggressive movements. I owe my life to the Don and so I took the responsibility seriously. I will never be anyone's son, and I will never head a great house, but you will Francis. So I was made to do what normal men would not or could not do. Know this as long as that fuck Gamborino has the power he has, your father, my Patron's life is in danger. They have tried twice now, but luck has been on your father's side. You too will be seen as future danger. They will be seeking revenge, so what choice do I have but take this war seriously. We have him finally in a position to make sure he fails, and he will be unable to control anything this powerful again. If my plan succeeds there will be a threat to the La Barba family no more. Nor to the many others, who their families he has had under their thumbs. In the long run the La Barba family will be heroes. The family's future is in my hands now but shortly you will have to step up when the Don is gone and so this choice should be yours. This decision effects whether La Barba trading companies are in the sulfur business or not?" Masso sat down and waited for a reply.

The two men sat across from each other, neither saying a word. Masso was thinking, *I hope he finally sees I am not* the *threat, but a preplanned solution.*

Francis is thinking, *he is right on many things he has said, but this is my opportunity to get rid of him once and for all. If he is really only in this for the La Barba family, this is my chance.* "What is in all this for Masso, if all you want to do is save the family and protect your Patron?"

Masso smiles, "Don't you see, it is so simple. My freedom, my obligation to the Don and this family will be over."

"You're telling me when this is done and the Alliance in place, you are going to just walk away, and not want to run the Alliance with your militia?"

"Yes that is exactly what I am saying, but for my men I want the Alliance to provide something for each one of them. Rizzo is to remain its secretary treasure. He is very smart with numbers and knows where to go and what to do, in order get things done. Divain is now Don of his own Laitfundia, and a member of the Alliance. This should not change. He has earned this, and is a very smart man as well and will be a good friend of your family if you let him. Gerome should be on a retainer; he can be reached and be here in two days when needed and totally loyal to the cause and will do whatever needs to be done. Charlie should get Molti

Soldi except the casino should kick back twenty five percent back to the Alliance just because it was the Alliances first investment so she should still get a little taste of the honey from her. Roberto should be given the Black Rose but there too, twenty five percent of the profits go back to the Alliance. Lastly my suggestion is that Alberto be given the soon to be bankrupted Gamborino Laitfundia, the family should be able to pick it up at a bargain. No one else will want to own the property with such bad spirits now running wild. I also suggested you encourage Alberto to become involved in politics. The family will need someone on the inside with political connections as time goes by. Work with your uncle and his boys they are good people too, family is the most important asset you have Francis whether you realize it or not. My tin men will be leaving soon, though if I were you, I would keep one around, they are very handy in handling sticky problems, but that's up to you. Last, spend time with your father, read some of his old journals it will give you a better insight to him and where he was coming from."

The answer did not come promptly but it did come. "If Albedo can salvage the marriage contract, and if you will sign an agreement to what you just said, we have a deal."

The two men shook hands for the first time. A deal was stuck.

Money for the wedding contract had already been deposited in the Goldins bank and notes prepare for bill of sales for all of Don' Philepo Delagleo tonnage. The due date came and went. The sure thing that Don Gamborino had gambled all his fortune on was called due and he could not produce. The terms of the contract were if the contract holder could not meet the called for tonnage, it could be purchased at last year's lowest price. The previous year's harvests were record breaking, so prices were down. This year's harvest was way off normal, making it harder for the gambler to control. The family did not have enough to pay the bankers and all of those orchards he had under contracts were also only paid last year's low prices.

The May wedding of Don Leonardo La Barba's son Francis La Barba to the daughter of Don Louis Narcis Miss Antonetta Narcis was the event of the year, invitations were actually being forged. They made a beautiful couple and both families were relieved.

The Alliances, [this thing of ours, would also be known as the Mafia in the future] membership grew in record time and its power to control the market grew and so the power of the Alliance spread, into the fabric of every business and most people's lives. All thanks to a small yellow sour fruit.

"Where are we off to now Masso my friend?"

"Anywhere this road takes us, Sir Poppy anywhere but here."

Principal Characters:

Tomasso Del La Rosa or better known as **Masso**, the **Bastardo,** who was breed for the job as Arbitrator for the La Barbra family.

Count Roberto La Barbra, a cousin of the King of Sicily, and the member of the family who received in the 1700's as a gift the property that would be known as Del La Rosa.

Georgeo La Barbra, Roberto's son, the man who successfully grew the estate to three times its original size and began the lemon orchards.

Arturo La Barbra, Georgeo's son, Leonardo's father. A drunk, philander and gambler.

Don Leonardo La Barbra, the owner of Del La Rosa, the families lemon orchard estate in Enna province Sicily and a growing businessman, with interest in sulfur mining, shipping and lemon trading. The senior member of the family, which included his younger brother Arturo and his three boys. The Dons only legal son Francis and the future inheritor.

Don Arturo La Barbra, Leonardo's younger brother. He has three children, Arturo the third, Alberto, and Antonio.

Arturo the third, nephew of Don Leonardo, a Captain in the Sardinian Army. AKA the army of Italy at the time.

Francis La Barbra, the Don Leonardo's legal heir, known screw up and influenced by his mother's two twin brothers, Marco and Paola Luccus.

Mella, the adopted mother of Masso. A herbalist and mid-wife, Don's Leonardo mistress in early years and later in life his care giver.

Augusto, Mell s husband and Masso's adopted father. The La Barbra families Arbitrator for a while.

Father Stefano Goldin, the areas Catholic priest, and the Don's adviser. His two brothers **Hector and Felix** were also the La Barbra families' bankers. The Goldin family who were Murano Jews passing as Catholics.

The **Allaya's** who control the area s water rights which most of the farms use to water their orchards.

Don Tito Delfino, large lemon orchard owner, who was Don Leonardo's close friend. Father of **Lucia and Enrico**.

Albert Rizzo was the quarter master in the Sardinian Army, and Masso's first recruit into the Special Forces he begins to train.

Divain, a well-educated member of Masso's trained Special Forces.

Charlie, a light hearted ladies' man and another member of Masso's trained Special Forces.

Gerome a large man with great strength, Charles friend and a key member of Masso's trained Special Forces.

Laurence Salvo AKA Sir Poppy Cock, flamboyant, animal groomer and a late arrival to Masso's group.

Roberto Rosso, hotel manager of the Black Rose Inn.

Don Ralphael Cheezo owner of the Sulphur mine the La Bara family has the lease on.

Paolo Cheezo, nephew of Don Raphael.

Braggio Narcisi, long term leaser of the Del LaRosa estate, black sheep of the very wealthy Narcisi family of Palermo.

Don Louis Narcis , head of the entire Narcis family, Braggio's uncle and Antonetta's father.

Antonetta Narcis, Francis La Barba's future wife.

Carmino Calderone proprietor of the Vizzini orchards, and a prize winning pig breeder. Father to **Agosto**, his son, and **Grazia** his daughter and husband **to Donna Vizzini Calderone**

Tin Men/ for hire assassins. Rose, Masso's biological mother is from this tribe. **Penelope** is Masso's grandmother and **Jaco** his uncle.

Alceu fa mily. The third wealthiest family in Catania Sicilly, Head of the family and its investments, is **Carmine Alceu. Son Gabbriel.**

Don Philepo Delagleo one of Sicily's largest lemon orchard owner.

Don Gamborino acting head of the Gamborino family, from Sampogna Sicily just outside of Palarmo. Large orchard owners and controlled a big part of the lemon business.

Deno Gamborino, the Don's male of the Gamborino family and rightful and legal heir to the Gamborino's ancient estate. The current acting Don's older brother.

Barlindo, the pregnant teen that Poppy won in dice game, from her father.

Places and locations:

Molti Soldi, gaming house **AKA Big Money**, owned by the Alliance, and located in the city of Pizza Sicily.

The Black Rose Inn, owned by Don La Barbra and run by Roberto Rosso, Masso's first test and victim.

Cascata del Diavulu / Waterfall of the Devil, Seasonal tourist attraction of spectator views of waterfalls **and** the base of the mountain range where the Tin Men live.

Sicilian term:

Vinnitta, Vendetta ..A deep rooted grudge.

Laitfundia, Large rural estates in Sicily who are owned by the Mother Church or absentee owners who live elsewhere.

Umoini Donare , Men of Honor, who ran the Laitfundia's for the owners. Collecting rents and solving problems on the estates for the land owners.

Luppa, short barrel shot gun.

Cummari, a Mistress.